When Roan looked at her again and their gazes met, he felt a connection to her so strong and powerful, it took his breath away. The magnetic pull was far stronger than even the most insistent sexual desire, more potent than any compulsion he'd ever had. Yet he couldn't close the gap between them, those few inches of cold air that represented a fathomless canyon.

He'd promised, dammit. He'd let her down before, and he would not—

"Roan." Victoria's voice was unsure. "You don't have to be a gentleman tonight if you don't want to."

He stared at her for several seconds, uncomprehending. Then all at once he understood what she was saying, and the enormity of it scared the hell out of him, almost swamping the red-hot desire coursing through his veins. Almost.

WHAT ARE *LOVESWEPT* ROMANCES?

They are stories of true romance and touching emotion. We believe those two very important ingredients are constants in our highly sensual and very believable stories in the LOVESWEPT *line. Our goal is to give you, the reader, stories of consistently high quality that may sometimes make you laugh, sometimes make you cry, but are always fresh and creative and contain many delightful surprises within their pages.*

Most romance fans read an enormous number of books. Those they truly love, they keep. Others may be traded with friends and soon forgotten. We hope that each LOVESWEPT *romance will be a treasure—a "keeper." We will always try to publish*

LOVE STORIES YOU'LL NEVER FORGET
BY AUTHORS YOU'LL ALWAYS REMEMBER

The Editors

HELL ON WHEELS

KAREN LEABO

BANTAM BOOKS
NEW YORK · TORONTO · LONDON · SYDNEY · AUCKLAND

HELL ON WHEELS

A Bantam Book / April 1996

LOVESWEPT and the wave design are registered trademarks of Bantam Books, a division of Bantam Doubleday Dell Publishing Group, Inc. Registered in U.S. Patent and Trademark Office and elsewhere.

ISBN 0-553-44541-3

Published simultaneously in the United States and Canada

Bantam Books are published by Bantam Books, a division of Bantam Doubleday Dell Publishing Group, Inc. Its trademark, consisting of the words "Bantam Books" and the portrayal of a rooster, is Registered in U.S. Patent and Trademark Office and in other countries. Marca Registrada. Bantam Books, 1540 Broadway, New York, New York 10036.

PRINTED IN THE UNITED STATES OF AMERICA

OPM 0 9 8 7 6 5 4 3 2 1

ONE

"This will fix you right up," Victoria Driscoll said as she set a bowl of her homemade chicken soup in front of Amos.

Amos snorted, pulling the afghan tighter around his burly shoulders. "Can it bring a body back from the dead?"

"Now, Professor, you're not that bad off."

"How would you know, missy? It's not your nasal passages that are involved."

As they both sat down at Amos's old metal kitchen table to eat the soup, Victoria had to admit the professor looked and sounded pretty bad. Gone was the youthful vigor that usually made him seem much younger than his sixty-eight years. His nose resembled a big Italian tomato stuck onto his face. His already gravelly voice sounded more and more like the grinding of a cement mixer with each passing hour. And he must be feeling as bad as he looked, if his temperament was any indication. Always a little gruff, today he was downright snappish.

"How's the soup?" she asked brightly. "I know, I'll make you some orange juice—" She started to get up, but Amos slapped his hand down on the tabletop.

"Victoria!"

"Yes?" she squeaked.

"Stop fussing. You're making me feel like some senile, feeble old fool. I'd like to believe this angel-of-mercy routine of yours comes from your sincere concern for my welfare—"

"I am concerned." She meant it. It scared her to see the ageless Professor Cullen looking suddenly like her grandfather.

"But you might not be *quite* so concerned if our chase trip weren't starting tomorrow."

Victoria settled back into her chair and propped her chin on her hand. "All right, yes, I do have an ulterior motive in seeing that you get well. I'm so antsy to get started on our trip, I can't stand it. We already missed that F-3 storm up in Guyman."

"And you'll likely miss a few more before you retire your video camera." Amos pushed his soup bowl aside. "Missy, I love a tornado as much as you, but if I leave this house anytime in the next week, it'll be in a pine box. I'm an old man, and I'm sick. I can't go chasing with you this time." He shook his head sadly. "Not this time."

Victoria sighed. "I'm sorry, Amos. Of course you can't jump up from a sickbed and spend sixteen hours a day in a car for two weeks straight." She was silent for a few moments as she thought about her options. "Maybe I could still switch my vacation. . . ."

"Now, missy, you don't think I'd leave you high and dry, do you? I've taken the liberty of finding you a substitute chase partner."

"What? Who?" she asked, automatically suspicious. She'd never considered chasing with anyone but Amos, a world-renowned tornado expert. His experience combined with his uncanny weather forecasting abilities, not to mention his impressive array of electronic gear, had always made her feel safe, even on those occasions when they came face-to-face with a killer storm. The idea of speeding around the countryside with anyone else gave her the heebie-jeebies.

"Now, hear me out. He's not a meteorologist, but he's had some experience with storms. He covered Hurricane Andrew for a South Carolina TV station, and, um, oh, yes, he was at that earthquake in Guatemala—"

"Oh, no! You aren't by any chance referring to that crazy nephew of yours, are you? What's his name—Ro . . . Ro-Something?"

"It's Roan, and he's not crazy, just . . . adventurous."

"He's a loose cannon!" Victoria insisted. "I watched that video he sent, remember? Good grief, the man stood on a beach during an F-6 hurricane. He almost got blown to kingdom come. And those other stories you've told me! He nearly cooked himself alive when he broke through two police barricades to get closer to that volcano in Japan. And didn't you tell me he almost got speared to death in Kenya when he photographed some elephant poachers?"

Amos actually chuckled. " 'Almost' is the key word."

"I'm not spending two weeks with him," she huffed.

"Now, missy, I've already invited him. He's driving in from Mississippi today. He was participating in some rafting race, I believe."

"Is there anything he hasn't participated in?"

"Yes. He's never seen a tornado." Amos touched Victoria's hand. "Victoria, let's be serious for a minute. I understand why you might be leery about chasing with someone like Roan. You're right, he isn't the most cautious person in the world. But I had more than one reason for inviting him."

"Other than to torture me, you mean?"

"Please, just listen for a minute," Amos continued, undaunted by Victoria's acid tongue. "My brother, Roan's father, was in the army and dragged his family all over the globe. Some kids have problems with that kind of upbringing, but Roan seemed to thrive on being constantly on the move. He saw every new environment as a challenge, a new world to be conquered. Nothing scared him. He was always the first to try a strange food or an unfamiliar game or sport. I rarely saw that kid when he wasn't smiling, excited about whatever he happened to be doing with his life at the time."

"Sounds like he was too good to be true."

"Your pessimism wounds me, Victoria. Roan was a pleasure to be around, even if he did keep his parents breathless with worry most of the time."

"I guess I can't blame them," Victoria said. "It's a miracle he's stayed in one piece all these years."

"Not really. He was always bold, but not foolhardy. He took calculated risks."

"You're talking in the past tense," Victoria pointed out.

Amos scratched his chin thoughtfully. "The last couple of years Roan has been taking more unreasonable chances. Before, he was simply unafraid. Now . . . I'm afraid he really does have a death wish."

Sensing Amos's pain, Victoria backed off from uttering the sarcastic remarks on the tip of her tongue. Amos was no stranger to death. His wife had died young, and he'd never remarried. He had no children of his own. A few years before, he'd lost a young niece to drowning—Roan's sister, she remembered now.

"Is there any reason Roan would have such flagrant disregard for his own life?" she asked.

"Well . . . he took Kim's death pretty hard, as we all did, but he's never seemed exactly depressed about it."

Victoria shook her head. When she'd lost her father, it had given her a keener appreciation of life. She couldn't see how the demise of a loved one would give anyone a death wish.

"Anyway," Amos continued, "we're all concerned about the boy, and I think you might be able to help."

"How?" she asked, once again suspicious.

Amos patted her arm affectionately. "You're no shrinking violet. You experience life fully, yet you have a strong survival instinct. Most people never see even one tornado. You've witnessed dozens, yet you never put yourself in any real danger. I thought that if Roan could spend some time with you, if you could show him a tornado or two, he would see that it's possible to feel all the excitement life has to offer without continually risking his neck."

Victoria fiddled with the end of her long, auburn braid. Amos was putting her in an awkward position. If she refused to go storm chasing with Roan Cullen, she would be insensitive to Amos's worries about his nephew. But if she agreed, she might be endangering herself. She had her own reasons for avoiding people who didn't hold a healthy respect for the power of a storm.

In the face of her indecision, Amos added the final, irresistible incentive: "I'll let you take the van."

Victoria's mouth dropped open. "You mean you'd actually let me drive the Chasemobile? Take it out of your sight?" In the year since he'd bought the minivan and loaded it up with a mind-boggling array of weather-sensing and communications equipment, he'd hardly let anyone else ride in it, much less drive it. Victoria couldn't blame him. He had well over thirty thousand dollars invested in the vehicle.

"I have complete faith in you, my girl. You're a good driver, and you keep your head during tense situations."

Victoria sipped another spoonful of soup. "I could call you from the road, I suppose, and get your forecasts—"

"Dang it, missy, what's the point of hauling around

that computer if you're going to hang on my apron strings? You can do your own forecasts."

Victoria went silent again. She had a master's degree in meteorology and a job as a forecaster for the National Weather Service. She was good at her job. But not as good as Amos. Just about anyone could analyze the data and come up with a general area where a storm might brew. But Amos could scan the horizon, sniff the breeze, and then drive with unveering certainty to the exact point at which the tornado would form. He knew the moods of a storm, where it would go, and how fast. That's why she'd always felt so safe with him.

Would she feel as safe relying on her own abilities?

"You'd better decide pretty quick," Amos said, " 'cause unless I miss my guess, that squeal of tires I hear means we're about to have company from Mississippi."

There was certainly nothing wrong with Amos's hearing, Victoria mused as, moments later, the crunch of gravel under tires and the shriek of brakes in need of new pads signaled the arrival of Roan Cullen.

"I'll get the door," she said just as the bell chimed.

"Victoria?" Amos stopped her. "Will you do it? As a favor to me, please. I can't think of anyone who could benefit more from your common sense and your reverence for life than my nephew."

She was not going to allow Amos to send her on a guilt trip. "I'll have to meet him first," she said, trying to sound sensible.

"Fair enough."

The bell chimed again, followed by a loud rapping

and a muffled voice. "Unc? You in there? Up and at 'em! Those tornadoes aren't going to wait for us, you know."

"Oh, Lord," Victoria murmured as she hurried to open the door.

The man standing on the front porch looked exactly as she'd pictured him—only worse. No, not worse, just . . . more. More rugged, more powerful, taller, broader, stronger, wilder. His loose khaki shorts were slung low on lean hips. His bright blue T-shirt, bearing the phrase I SURVIVED THE RIVER RAT RACE, COLDWATER, MISSISSIPPI hugged his wide shoulders and bulging biceps. His hair was on the long side, hanging almost to his shoulders in untamed waves of caramel brown streaked gold from the sun, and it hadn't seen a comb in a while.

Most disturbing were his eyes, a vivid, piercing blue assessing her boldly from his lean, weather-whipped face. He was almost intimidating—until he suddenly smiled, and tiny crinkles appeared at the corners of those alarming eyes and a dimple formed at the corner of his arrogantly upturned mouth.

"So, at long last, I get to meet the infamous Victoria Driscoll." He extended his hand, and Victoria took it automatically, acutely aware of the power in his casual grasp, the long, tanned fingers wrapping around hers.

"You must be Roan," she said coolly, not at all sure she liked his assessment. "And I'd say that between the two of us, if anyone's infamous, it's you. I'm surprised you've even heard of me."

"Oh, everyone in the Cullen family knows about you. Years ago we all thought you were a gold digger, but I guess if that were true, you would have either married Amos or left for greener pastures. Can I come in?"

Victoria could only stare in openmouthed shock. The man was unforgivably rude. In the first place, Amos wasn't exactly a prime target for a gold digger. He lived in a two-bedroom frame house in a modest neighborhood of Lubbock, Texas. He was a tenured professor at Texas Tech University, so he had some security, but he was hardly rich. In the second place, Amos was her friend and mentor, nothing more. Anyone who thought otherwise was an ignorant fool.

Well, at least Roan Cullen had admitted that his assumption was mistaken. Figuring the best defense was to ignore his tactless comment, she stood aside to let him in.

"It's hotter than hell in here," Roan said. "Is the AC broken?"

"It's warm in here because Amos has a fever and he was chilled," she said, closing the door.

"A fever?" Roan's eyebrows drew together in a frown. "Is he okay?"

"Get in here, boy, and I'll show you okay," Amos called irritably from the kitchen. "Can't stand it when people talk behind my back."

Victoria shrugged and led the way to the kitchen. She had already made up her mind—she wouldn't go on the road with Roan Cullen. She needed to think clearly and act sensibly while she was chasing. With Roan around, she was sure she could do neither.

Karen Leabo
10

"So, what's this about a fever?" Roan asked as he strode into the kitchen to find his uncle sitting at the table, hunched over a bowl of soup.

"It's not just a fever, it's the cold from hell," Amos grumbled. "And if you don't want to catch it, you'll keep your distance."

"I never get sick," Roan argued, leaning down to give the old man a hug. Amos was one of Roan's favorite relatives. They rarely saw each other these days, and Roan wasn't about to keep his distance.

"Amos, can I warm that soup up for you?" Victoria offered.

Roan turned his attention to the woman who'd answered the door. He had known she would be coming with them on their trip; Amos apparently never chased without her, not since his former chase partner had retired four years earlier. But Roan hadn't expected to find her firmly entrenched in Amos's house, playing hostess.

When she'd answered the door she'd been so cool and regal, looking down her nose at him, judging him, that he hadn't been able to resist saying something outrageous to shake her composure—which he had. But he'd never really believed her to be after Amos's money, not even all those years ago, when the rest of the family was all fired up about this coed Amos had become so fond of. Amos had more sense than to be taken in by a pretty face.

But Roan hadn't been prepared for her to be *so*

pretty—tall and slender, with a classic cameo face, large hazel eyes, and thick russet hair pulled into a demure braid that trailed halfway down her back. The moment he'd laid eyes on her, he'd wondered what her hair would look like loose, falling over her shoulders. Bare shoulders.

Not that she was Roan's type. He liked women with easy smiles, the kind who flirted and teased and ultimately gave in, the kind who played hard and were willing to put up with his rather lackadaisical approach to commitment. Victoria Driscoll, he suspected, was none of those things. And yet she was intriguing, perhaps the type a staid older man would fall for.

Roan wondered. She certainly moved about the kitchen with ease, as if she were accustomed to it.

"Would you like some soup, Roan?" she asked, all politeness.

"You should try it," Amos said. "Victoria made it herself. She's a marvelous cook."

"Well, in that case I'd love some. Haven't eaten since lunch, four hours ago." His smile was met with cool complacency. Maybe he shouldn't have made that gold-digger crack. He'd meant only to tease her, not turn her into a permanent enemy.

"There's beer in the fridge, and some cold cuts," Amos said. "If I know you, you'll want something more substantial than soup."

"Thanks, I think I will. It was a long, hot drive from Mississippi."

"How did the raft race go?" Amos asked. "You win?"

Roan laughed easily. "There were almost two hundred entrants. I was in the lead for a while, but then I hit a snag in some white water. The milk jugs got hung up on—"

"Milk jugs?" Victoria asked, pausing in the middle of ladling soup into a bowl.

"The rafts had to be homemade to qualify." He located salami, bologna, ham, and cheese in the refrigerator, along with some onion rolls. With practiced efficiency he began assembling a sandwich. "I floated old tires on a base of empty milk jugs. It was a damn good design too. I would have won if I hadn't gotten caught up on those rocks."

"Well, you can't win 'em all," Amos said.

"I came in third. Won a two-hundred-dollar prize, and a documentary production company bought my film, so it wasn't a total loss." He took his sandwich to the table and sat down at the place Victoria had set for him. She put a steaming bowl of soup in front of him without comment.

Well, it was a cinch his rafting exploits weren't impressing her, which was rather refreshing. He sampled the soup. "Mmm, this is great, Vicky."

A cold wave seemed to descend on the room, and Roan knew darn well no one had turned on the air-conditioning. Everyone grew very still.

"My name's Victoria, not Vicky," she said, her voice crisp.

"Oh, sorry. I'll try to remember, but nicknames just sort of pop out of my mouth. Most people like them, right, Unc?"

13

"I don't," she said.

Amos frowned disapprovingly, but Roan wasn't sure whether his uncle was displeased with him, with Victoria, or both of them.

"So, what time do we leave tomorrow?" Roan asked, diplomatically changing the subject.

Amos laid down his spoon. "Roan, in case you haven't noticed, I'm hanging on to life by a thread. My sinuses are on fire, my eyes are practically swelled shut, and my lungs sound like a calliope. I'm also running a hundred-and-one-degree fever, last I checked. I'm not going anywhere for at least a week."

"You mean you're canceling the trip?" Roan's disappointment was keen. Although he wouldn't have minded a day or two to recharge his batteries, the thought of canceling the whole trip depressed him. For years he'd wanted to go storm chasing with his uncle, and this was the first time Amos had ever consented to let him come along. He might not ever get another chance to see a tornado up close and personal.

"No, not exactly. You and Victoria can go without me. She needs a chase partner and you need a guide. The arrangement should work out perfectly—provided, of course, that Victoria agrees." Amos exchanged a meaningful look with his protégé.

Roan could have kicked himself clear to Katmandu. Now he really regretted the gold-digger comment, and he shouldn't have called her Vicky either. His fate rested in her hands, and judging from the black looks she kept aiming his way, the prognosis wasn't good.

Karen Leabo

14

"I'll get my stuff from the car," Roan announced decisively. He left the kitchen, but not before giving Victoria a long, almost challenging look.

She was glad to see him go. She would be relieved of his overwhelming presence for a few minutes anyway.

"You could at least be civil to the man," Amos scolded.

"Civil? He's lucky I didn't 'accidentally' dump that soup down the front of his shirt. He called me a gold digger!"

Amos's bushy white eyebrows drew together in an expression of incredulity. "Gold digger! Good Lord, I thought I'd laid that stupid rumor to rest years ago."

"It's okay," Victoria said quickly, before the professor got all excited and worked himself into another coughing attack. "He corrected himself. Said if I was after your money, I would have married you by now or moved on."

Amos laughed uproariously at that, prompting a series of hacking coughs anyway. "And what a catch I'd be too," he said when he'd recovered. "Don't worry, missy, I think Roan was just rattling your cage. He doesn't mean any harm. You'll take him along, won't you?"

Victoria tried not to look at Amos, at those hopeful, red-rimmed eyes. After all he'd done for her, how could she turn down such an earnest request? "I haven't decided," she said once again. "Amos, can you in good conscience send me off for two weeks alone with your nephew? At the very least he'll drive me crazy. At the worst he'll distract me so badly I'll make a dumb decision and get us both killed."

"Now, missy, I've never seen you get even a little rattled during a chase, and I don't believe you'll start now, no matter how, er, distracting my nephew might be."

"Distracting" didn't even begin to describe Roan Cullen, Victoria thought.

"Besides," Amos continued, "he might turn out to be a better chase partner than you think. I'll wager he's a great navigator, and you can't argue with his photographic skills. He'll blow both of us away in that area."

"Please, let's not talk about getting blown away."

Amos chuckled briefly, but then his expression grew somber. "If you don't want to chase with Roan, I suppose I could find someone else for him to ride with. Those two kids from the university, John Higgenbotham and Dave Devors. They're always looking for someone to finance their chase trips, and I'll warrant Roan would front the money."

Victoria shivered at the thought of those three on the road together. "John and Dave? Neither of them can forecast their way out of a paper bag, and when they're lucky enough to find a storm, their main objective seems to be to punch right through the middle of it and do as much damage to their car as possible."

Amos frowned. "Hmm, you're right. Roan would only encourage them to be irresponsible. Any other suggestions?"

"What about Eddie and Marilyn Dunne?"

Amos shook his head. "I wouldn't do that to Eddie.

You know how Marilyn is. She likes to chase something besides storms, and she'd be on Roan like mold on cheese." Amos sighed. "Oh, well, maybe next year. I hope he doesn't decide to take off on his own to chase storms. He knows just enough about it to get himself in real trouble."

Victoria couldn't stand to hear the defeat in Amos's voice. "Oh, all right!" she said, wondering what she was getting herself into. "I'll give it a try. But if Roan doesn't behave himself, I'm coming straight home."

Amos beamed. "That's my girl. I knew you wouldn't let me down."

They suspended their conversation when Roan came back inside carrying a cardboard box full of dirty laundry. "Okay if I use your washer and dryer, Unc?" he asked.

"Sure. It's out on the back porch."

"I remember."

Victoria watched him walk through the kitchen. She couldn't help herself. He had a certain aura about him that drew the female eye. It wasn't just his taut body either. It was more a sense of quiet but dangerous layers that hid just below the happy-go-lucky surface.

She realized Amos was talking to her.

". . . leave the dishes and go watch the Weather Channel. I want to see what's cooking for tomorrow."

They sat together on the couch in the living room. Amos made notes on the photocopied blank maps he always kept at the ready. Victoria stared at the screen, but her attention was on the sound of running water and off-key whistling coming from the back porch.

"Just one thing I should warn you about," Amos said quietly, his eyes on the screen as he penciled in fronts, wind direction, and high and low pressure zones.

"Just one?" she said dryly.

"No matter what happens, don't let Roan drive."

TWO

It felt great to indulge in a real, hot shower, Roan thought as the stinging spray pelted his shoulders and cascaded down his body. Before the raft race, he'd been on assignment for *National Geographic*, camping in West Virginia with a group of scientists studying black bears. Baths in a nearby river, plus an occasional shave with a battery-powered razor, had kept him reasonably well-groomed, but nothing could compare to a close shave and the hot spray and steam from good ol' indoor plumbing. This was the second shower he'd taken since his arrival in Lubbock the day before.

He didn't even mind the razor nick he'd inflicted on his chin.

When he emerged from the bathroom, he heard voices coming from Amos's office, otherwise known as "Tornado Central," and he meandered to the open doorway to see what was going on. Amos and Victoria were hunched over a group of maps, seeming to do battle with handfuls of colored markers. Their conversation made little sense to Roan; something about "convergence" and "diffluence" and "upper-level wind velocities" and "millibars," whatever those were. They'd been arguing good-naturedly since Victoria's arrival an hour before.

"So, how's it look?" he asked.

They both turned, and he found he liked the way Victoria stared and her cheeks pinkened.

"Roan, for heaven's sake, put some clothes on," Amos blustered. "There's a lady present."

Yes, Victoria was a lady all right, a class act down to her indigo jeans, obviously new, and cotton blouse with little rosebuds embroidered on the collar. Only a true lady would blush at a man wrapped fairly decently in a towel. "What kind of clothes should I put on?" he asked innocently. "I wasn't sure what was appropriate for storm chasing."

"Anything comfortable," Victoria answered, quickly recovering her poise. "We'll spend most of our time in the car. And bring a jacket." She turned her attention back to her maps.

He had a long way to go before winning over Ms. Victoria Driscoll, he realized, looking forward to the challenge. At least she hadn't decided to cancel the trip. If she were willing to spend two weeks in a car alone with him, she must not despise him too thoroughly.

He retreated to the guest room and plucked a pair of tiger-striped briefs from a pile of freshly washed laundry. "For you, Vicky," he murmured, grinning.

He wasn't planning to make a play for her; Amos

would knock him silly for even thinking about it. But she was an intriguing package, so solemn and scientific. He couldn't imagine what she was hiding behind those changeable hazel eyes. Trying to guess would give him something to think about during the long hours in the car to come.

After climbing into his oldest, most faded pair of jeans and another T-shirt from his almost endless supply, he quickly folded several changes of clothes and stuck them in his duffel, along with his travel kit. If there was one thing he could do quickly and efficiently, it was pack. His camera equipment would take up more room than his clothing.

He stopped long enough to run a comb through his wet hair, ruthlessly pulling out several tangles. How long had it been since he'd really examined himself in the mirror? he wondered. He was leaning a bit toward the caveman look, but he supposed there wouldn't be time for a haircut today. It was past nine o'clock. He was surprised they weren't already on the road, but Victoria hadn't behaved as if she were in any particular hurry.

He carried his things out and set them by the front door, ready to roll at a moment's notice, then checked in again with Tornado Central. Amos and Victoria were now staring at a radar display on a television set, discussing something about a slow-moving front and a dry line and where the "triple point" was likely to be by midafternoon. Another weather map was displayed on Amos's computer.

"So, how does it look?" Roan asked for the second time. He never really got an answer the first go-round.

"Pretty marginal," Amos said.

"Dismal," Victoria added.

"Does that mean we're not going?" Roan was surprised at the pang of disappointment he felt. Only yesterday he'd been wishing for a couple of days off to recharge his batteries. But today he found himself eager to be on the road again.

"Oh, we'll go," Victoria said resignedly. "We might be taking pictures of cactuses and lizards instead of tornadoes, but there's always a chance."

"Yeah, there's always a chance," Roan repeated, holding eye contact with her.

Her eyes widened slightly, as if she couldn't quite believe her ears or the cocky, flirtatious grin he gave her. She stared at him so long, in fact, his grin faded and he was the one who looked away first.

"Your chin is bleeding," she said.

"Mmm." He grabbed a tissue from the box Amos carried everywhere with him, and dabbed unconcernedly at the shaving nick. "Is there time for breakfast?"

"More time than we need," Victoria said. "I made some bran muffins this morning. They're in the kitchen. There's orange juice too."

"Bran muffins?" Roan repeated with just a touch of skepticism as he stood aside to let the other two exit the office.

Amos surreptitiously punched him in the arm with more force than a sick old man ought to be capable of. But it caught Roan's attention and prevented him from adding, *Blech*. What he wanted for breakfast were some eggs and bacon, pancakes, maybe French toast, but that didn't mean he ought to insult Victoria's offering. Given her underwhelming enthusiasm for his company, she might be looking for any reason to call off the whole trip.

The muffins, laced with cranberries, weren't half bad, especially with a heavy coating of butter and three cups of coffee to wash them down. But Roan still craved a healthy dose of cholesterol. After camping with those bear-watching people, who acted as if they'd never heard of refined sugar, caffeine, or white flour, much less alcohol or tobacco, he'd had it up to the gills with healthy living.

"Well, I guess we ought to get on the road," Victoria said with a baleful face. She looked like she was headed for a jail sentence instead of her vacation.

Amos ceremoniously handed her the keys to his van. "Take good care of her."

"I'll be careful. And if there's any damage, I'll pay for it."

"Oh, now, missy, that's not necessary. It's about time Chasemobile II got christened with a few hail dents. Just"—his gaze darted toward Roan and back—"just remember what I said."

Roan knew Amos's veiled reference had something to do with him, but he chose to let it pass. Amos had probably warned Victoria not to let Roan take advantage of her, or some such nonsense. Amos was awfully protective of his protégé, even if they weren't romantically involved.

23

"This is some fancy equipment you have here," Victoria commented as they loaded Roan's things into the back of the van. He certainly hadn't scrimped when it came to his video camera, which was an even more recent model than Amos's.

"It's my living. I try to stay up-to-date, except for that old Nikon. It was made back before everything went electronic. No bells or whistles, but it's the best camera for a flood or rainstorm. It won't short out if it gets wet."

"Like in a hurricane?" She pointedly eyed his HURRICANE ANDREW BLEW ME AWAY T-shirt, noticing the way the thin red cotton stretched across his chest and the sleeves rode up high on his biceps. The thing had obviously shrunk in the wash. Surely he hadn't bought it that snug on purpose.

Or maybe he had. She had to drag her gaze away.

"Most of my pictures of Andrew were taken from inside a car," he replied, seemingly oblivious of her appraisal. "You ever seen a hurricane?"

"No, and I don't plan to. There's no challenge chasing a hurricane. You always know where it is. Anyone who can't get out of the way of one is just asking for trouble, in my opinion." She knew she was being too critical of him, and she vowed to watch herself more closely in the future. Her job was to gently prod Roan to see things her way—not antagonize him.

He didn't seem to take offense. "Maybe so, but nothing compares to a firsthand encounter with those one-hundred-sixty-mile-per-hour winds. As a meteorologist, wouldn't you like to experience that?"

She actually shivered, despite the fact that the heat of a West Texas day was already building. She'd watched Roan's hurricane videos—roofs and billboards flying through the air, palm trees bent almost to the ground, people fleeing for their lives.

Watching the video, she'd felt for a minute that she was actually in the middle of all that violence, bringing back painful, frightening memories.

"I wouldn't," she finally answered. "The study of storms is strictly a spectator sport for me. I don't like getting in the middle of one, and I never will."

"Oh." He actually looked disappointed. Maybe the man did have a death wish, as Amos feared.

Of course, Roan had no idea how ferocious a tornado could be. Although much smaller than hurricanes, tornadoes could pack more punch, driving metal through wood, picking up cars—and tractors—and carrying them hundreds of feet into the air. At least with a hurricane, people knew it was coming and could get out of harm's way.

Not always so with a tornado.

Shaking off her grim thoughts, Victoria slammed shut the back doors of the van. "Ready?"

"Ready, but can we make one stop before leaving town? I need to return my rental car. Is there a Pennywise office around here?"

Victoria stared openmouthed at his gray midsized four-door sitting in the driveway. "That's a rental car?"

"Yeah. You don't think I'd own something that ugly, do you?"

Victoria owned a similar model, which was tucked away in Amos's garage, but she decided not to tell Roan that. "Did they rent it to you in that condition?"

"What condition? It runs great."

"I mean the broken headlight, cracked windshield, crumpled fender, missing hubcaps . . ."

"Oh, that. I did some pretty hard driving the last couple of weeks."

Couple of weeks? Amos wasn't kidding when he'd warned her not to let Roan drive. "There's a Pennywise office on the way out of town."

Amos was standing on the front porch, watching their preparations. Victoria went over to give him a farewell hug. "Take care of yourself, now," she said. "I'll really miss you."

"Somehow, I kind of doubt that," he replied with a wink. "A couple of young people with two weeks and endless stretches of highway ahead of them don't need an old man around."

Victoria started to object to his assessment, but he shushed her.

"Roan really means no harm," he said in a low voice. "Give him a chance. He'll settle down, and I bet the two of you will have a good time."

"Don't most men settle down after they leave their teenage years?" she whispered back. But she softened the question with a smile. She didn't want Amos worrying too much about her.

Even Roan gave Amos a quick hug and a blithe

promise that they would be careful. With one last wave and a honk of the van's horn, they were off—toward what, Victoria wasn't sure.

Roan followed her in his car to the Pennywise office. Well, followed wasn't exactly accurate. He apparently didn't like lagging behind anyone, so he alternated between tailgating her and pulling up into the lane next to her. He shot through one yellow light while she was able to stop in plenty of time, and he had to pull over and wait.

"Serves you right," she murmured. When the light turned green, she accelerated with deliberate slowness.

He spent an undue amount of time in the rental car office—probably trying to explain away the damage. When he came out, he held up one finger, indicating she should wait one minute, and then he sprinted across the parking lot to the convenience store next door. When he joined her a couple of minutes later, he had a big white bag.

"Fuel," he explained as he extracted a large coffee and two paper-wrapped sandwiches that appeared to be sausage and cheese. "The bran muffins were great, but I need something a little more substantial. I have a fast metabolism—burn up food as quickly as I can put it away."

Victoria didn't doubt it. He wasn't a small man, and there wasn't an ounce of fat evident on his body. All that muscle probably did burn up a lot of calories. That was another reason to dislike him. He could eat all he wanted and never get fat. Not that she had much of a problem in that area, but only because she worked hard at maintaining a healthful diet and getting plenty of exercise.

He extended one of the sandwiches in her direction. "You can have one if you want."

"No, thanks," she said with a delicate shudder. She appreciated his generosity, but from the looks of them, those sausages would supply a body with a year's worth of grease. She put the van into gear. "Fasten your seat belt, please."

For a moment she thought he was going to argue with her, but then he relented and slid the harness over his shoulder, fastening it with a resounding click. He looked about as comfortable as a lion wearing a leash.

"You don't like seat belts?" she asked, amazed that anyone in this day and age would object to wearing one.

"I don't like restraints. I'm sort of claustrophobic. Besides, I figure, when my number's up, it's up."

"That's one way to look at it," she agreed. "I'm not so worried about dying though. It's the living that scares me—sustaining a serious head injury and then living. In a nursing home."

"I'm wearing the seat belt, okay?" he said a trifle impatiently.

She actually managed to smile at him. "Sorry. I tend to get a little preachy sometimes. One of my most annoying habits. I'll try to control myself—oh, please don't spill any crumbs! The professor is very particular about his van."

Roan caught a crumb on the end of his finger before it could hit the upholstery. "I guess that means smoking is out of the question."

She bit her tongue to keep from gasping. "You smoke?"

"Sometimes. I'll keep it to a minimum if it annoys you."

"It annoys me only because I hate to see anyone—" she cut herself off midlecture. Roan Cullen was no child. Unless he lived under a rock, which apparently he didn't, he knew the dangers of smoking. "Just not in the van, please. Elsewhere you can do as you like."

He nodded. "No problem. And your control is admirable. I can tell you're dying to lecture."

"I'm sure you've heard it all. There's no need for me to repeat it." She forced herself to sound serene.

The first five minutes in the van with Roan were the most difficult. Driving the unfamiliar vehicle hadn't seemed such a chore until she had to do it with him watching every move she made. Even when his attention was focused innocently out the window, she was uncomfortably aware of his presence, his heat, the smell of shampoo from his still-damp hair. She hopped over a curb as she made too sharp a turn, then almost ran a red light. She wondered if she was even less qualified than Roan to drive Amos's precious van.

They had left the city behind them by the time Roan had finished his brunch. "So, where are we heading?" he asked.

She handed him a much-abused road atlas. "For now, our target is Odessa, maybe Monahans. We'll stop after noon and get some updated data, see if things are going as Amos predicted. But don't get your hopes up. I don't expect any decent storms until Monday or Tuesday."

"That's two or three days from now. What do we do in the meantime?"

That mischievous gleam in his eye made her nervous. Well, two could play at this game. Did he think she was such a prude, she could do nothing but stammer and blush at his little innuendos? "We drive and hope we get lucky."

He didn't seem to notice her choice of words. "I'm all for that," he said. Then he nodded toward the row of tuners mounted between the bucket seats. "Why don't you tell me what all this hardware does? That's clever, installing a video camera on the dash so you can tape and drive at the same time. But what about all this other stuff? Looks like you wiped out a Radio Shack."

She was relieved to change the subject. "These are ham radios. In every area of the country, ham operators are trained as storm spotters. They report hail, high winds, etcetera, to a network controller, who forwards the information to the Weather Service, and we can listen in. I can also pick up weather radio and AM stations. This is a police scanner. And that's a color TV. I guess you figured that out."

"And the computer in the back?" he asked, his eyes alight with interest.

"With the aid of a cellular phone and a modem, I can hook up to a Weather Service computer on the East Coast and get updated data every two hours. Then I use a software program to analyze the raw numbers and turn them into maps. That's what Amos and I were doing this morning."

Roan said nothing for a while, but he continued to study the equipment. Victoria tensed as he began fiddling with knobs and buttons, but she didn't stop him. Some men were just natural-born fiddlers. After a long silence he murmured, "Amazing."

"We like to take advantage of the latest technology. Some of the purists don't like it—they say we're taking all the romance out of the chase. They would rather get a morning weather report, sniff the air, and be off. But I don't chase for the romance."

"Then why do you do it?" he asked.

The question, accompanied by a penetrating stare, took her off guard. Over the years plenty of people had asked her why she chased, but a pat answer had always sufficed. She sensed that Roan Cullen wouldn't be satisfied with that.

"Well . . . I'm primarily a forecaster. It's gratifying to me when I make a prediction, then verify it firsthand."

"You could verify a prediction by watching the weather on television. And if you were interested merely in your accuracy, you would be just as gratified to predict a blizzard or a . . . a sunny day and be right. There must be some reason you deliberately seek out tornadoes, and only tornadoes. It couldn't be that you actually get a thrill from the danger, could it?"

"No," she said sharply. "You couldn't be further from the truth. Tornadoes are rare events, not like sunny days or even blizzards. To be able to predict accurately when and where one will occur—well, no one can do it with any consistency. But we're getting better at it all the time. My goal is to learn as much as I can, so I can be the best possible forecaster."

"And the thrill of the chase has nothing to do with it?" he asked with a skeptical lifting of one eyebrow.

"Oh, all right. I guess I do like the excitement of being so close to something so powerful. But my first priority is keeping myself and others safe from harm. The more I learn, the safer I am. I've witnessed almost thirty twisters, and I've never been hurt, or even close to it."

Not counting her first tornado.

If she'd known then what she knew now, she might have been able to change the outcome. But she seldom discussed her first, worst encounter with a twister, and she certainly didn't know Roan Cullen well enough to trust him with those most personal details of her life. Not even Amos knew about the killer storm that had convinced her to pursue meteorology as a career.

Roan nodded, seeming to digest her words. It was only afterward that she realized she was doing exactly what Amos had hoped she would do—impress upon Roan that life could be exciting without being dangerous. Whether he would take her advice was anybody's guess.

Roan was really curious now. She was hiding more behind those pretty hazel eyes than he could have guessed. Most of the women who'd flitted in and out of his life were the open-book variety—honest, up-front, no secrets, as obvious about their wants and needs as they were about their sexuality.

Victoria was the complete opposite—subtle, mysterious, her motives deeply hidden. At first he'd thought it would be fun to figure her out, to tease her out of her reticence. But it appeared the task wouldn't be so simple. She was a woman of layers. Peeling them off, one by one, to find the core would be a fascinating activity, but perhaps an impossible one. She had yet to respond to his attempts at charm, although that little smile she'd awarded him after her seat-belt lecture was enough incentive to make him want to try harder with her.

He should have asked Amos more about his protégé. Armed with a little information, Roan wouldn't have felt so out of his depth.

At half past noon Victoria pulled into a gas station to fill up the van. Roan handed her a twenty, which she accepted gracefully with murmured thanks. He might be a slight inconvenience to her, but at least he would carry his weight. He even pumped the gas while she ran inside to pay.

"Could you get me a Coke?" he called to her. Although the inside of the van was cool and comfortable, outside it was like a desert, quickly calling up a thirst.

She nodded before disappearing inside.

While the gas was pumping, Roan wandered to the edge of the parking lot and lit up his first cigarette of the day. He'd taken only a couple of drags when he heard the gas pump click, indicating the tank was full. He stamped out the cigarette, not wanting to cause a delay, but he wondered when his next chance to have one would be.

A few minutes later Victoria reappeared with a Coke for Roan and a bottle of mineral water for herself. She pulled the van onto a side street under a shady tree and stopped again. Leaving the motor running, she got out, came around to the sliding side door, and climbed back in.

Roan moved to the seat next to Victoria's and watched as her graceful hands flew over the laptop computer keyboard, logging on to the Weather Service computer on the East Coast.

Streams of numbers and letters flew across the color monitor, and in moments everything was downloaded. Victoria severed the phone connection, printed out the data on a quiet inkjet printer, then began the laborious task of interpretation.

She was quiet as she worked, giving Roan no indication as to whether the data were good or bad. He soon grew bored with watching the colorful maps she manipulated on the monitor, pretty though they were, and began studying Victoria herself.

She was oblivious of his inspection, and so he let his gaze wander lingeringly over her, liking what he saw more and more. He liked her delicate ears, graced with understated pearl stud earrings. He liked the little mole at the corner of her mouth. He especially liked how the wind had pulled several wisps of her rich reddish-brown hair free of her braid.

The door to the van had been left open, and the breeze whipped inside from time to time, causing those free wisps of hair to tickle her cheeks and forehead. She was so intent, her hands so busy, that she couldn't be bothered to brush the stray wisps aside, but Roan could tell she was annoyed by them.

If he'd thought for half a second, he never would have done it. The problem was, most of the time he didn't think before he spoke or moved, which often got him into trouble. This particular time he smoothed the strands of hair off Victoria's face.

He'd hardly completed the gesture, when he jerked his hand back, realizing what he'd done. He expected her to buck at the shock of his inappropriate touch, but she didn't. Instead, her fingers stilled on the keyboard and she turned slowly to look at him, her eyes wary.

"What are you doing?" Her voice quavered slightly.

He held both hands up in a gesture of surrender. "Your hair was in your face, and it was bothering you. I didn't mean anything by it, Vicky, honest. It was making my nose itch, watching those little wispies tickle you like that. I didn't think about what I was doing. It was instinctual."

She continued to stare, her breathing rapid and audible. After a few moments it slowed, and she looked down at her hands, still poised on the keyboard. "My name's Victoria."

He was puzzled by her response until he realized what she was talking about. "Oh, now, you see there? That's a perfect example. I didn't mean to call you Vicky, it just popped out of my mouth. I had a teacher once who said I must be missing a part of my brain, the part that edits what I say and do."

"You mean like good judgment?"

He could have sworn he saw just a trace of amusement dancing in her eyes, and he began to believe he might not have to hitchhike back to Lubbock after all. "Well, yeah, maybe that's it. But I have great judgment as long as I have time to think." Like now. He suddenly wanted to kiss her, but a little voice of reason told him that might not be such a hot idea at that moment. Definitely good judgment.

She released a long sigh. "Okay, let's just forget it. Do you want to see what I've been doing here?"

"Sure." He dutifully gazed at the computer screen.

"We're actually not in as bad a shape as I thought. See how the winds are circulating around these two low pressure areas? That's where the hot and cool air masses are meeting."

Roan studied the map. One area she indicated was northwest of them in New Mexico, a good two hundred miles. The other was southwest, about the same distance—almost in Big Bend country. "Which way do we head?"

Victoria chewed on her fingernail. "I don't know."

"Well, we'd better flip a coin, then."

She made no comment as she shut down the computer. She climbed out of the van and looked up at the sky. "See the thin layer of cirrus clouds moving in? That's good. It means that a warm, moist tongue is moving in from the gulf to feed moisture into the storms."

Warm, moist tongue, huh? He bit his own tongue so hard, he drew blood. Did she have any idea what words like that, coming from her, did to him? Obviously not, because she was still expounding on the clouds and upper level wind velocities.

". . . I guess maybe we should head back north, toward Raton," she said, though she sounded anything but sure of herself. "That way, if nothing comes of it, we'll at least be in a more central location for tomorrow. Besides, the farther south we go, the more mountains we'll get into and the worse the visibility will be."

"Sounds good to me," Roan said. He didn't care which direction they went, so long as they got moving. He wanted to turn on the van's air conditioner, although he doubted even a blast of arctic air would cool him down anytime soon.

THREE

Victoria silently second-guessed herself for the next hour and a half. What if she were wrong? She was strongly tempted to call Amos and ask him, but he'd made it clear that he wanted her to rely on her own forecasting abilities this time. Besides, she didn't want to wake him if he was resting.

Roan, apparently oblivious of her dilemma, kept up a running commentary about the West Texas landscape. She had to admit he was pretty entertaining, considering there wasn't all that much to look at—flat land dotted with pale green sagebrush, a few cattle, windmills, and oil wells. Sometimes the harsh land wrinkled up into little hills and canyons, only to flatten out again. With the exception of the two-lane blacktop highway, few signs of civilization were evident, hardly even a passing car.

"It's so deserted out here, we could be the last people on earth," he said. "Maybe we are. Maybe everyone else got sucked into space by the gravitational pull of a giant meteor."

"Oh, that would be terrible," she said with a melodramatic hand to her forehead. "How will we get our weather reports if everyone else is stuck to a meteor?"

"Seriously, I've flown back and forth between the coasts all my life," he said, "but other than occasional visits with Amos, I never spent much time in the middle of the country before."

"And now you see why," Victoria added with a knowing grin. "There's not much here."

"I wasn't going to say that. In fact, I find the emptiness kind of awe-inspiring. It'd be a great place to take pictures. I've never seen so much blue sky."

"We have great visibility in this part of the country, I'll give you that. When a tornado comes through, there's not much for it to hit. I'd much rather follow a storm out here than through a densely populated area."

"Damn, look at the size of that hawk. I sure would like to stop and take a few pictures."

She shook her head. "We don't have time to waste. The storms won't wait for us, you know."

"Has anyone ever told you you have a one-track mind?"

He'd said it with a teasing note in his voice, but Victoria didn't appreciate the comment. Probably because he was right. But keeping her attention focused firmly on weather matters was better than the alternative—thinking about him. And he was hard not to think about.

"I'm on this trip for one purpose, yes," she said in

her most businesslike tone, "and that's to find tornadoes."

"Are you always this intense about it?"

"You haven't begun to see intense. Anyway, this has been a slow season. I might get only one good shot this trip, and I don't intend to blow it."

"Oh." He paused, and she sensed he was poising himself for another assault. "Does that mean you actually are capable of carrying on a conversation that doesn't have something to do with the weather?"

"I have other interests," she objected.

"Really? Like what?"

He was doing it again, flirting with her—no, seducing her with that voice of his. There was nothing wrong with his question; it was how he said it, the expression on his face.

"I have a lot of interests—cooking, and . . . and gardening. I belong to a garden club."

His mellow laugh didn't irk her as much as it should have. "Is that where a bunch of little old ladies in hats and white gloves get together for tea and to show off their prize roses?"

"Not at all. It's an organic gardening club, and a lot of members are men."

His expression grew thoughtful. "I see. You must meet a lot of men, then."

"I beg your pardon?"

"Amos told me you're one of the few women who chase storms—one of the few in meteorology, for that matter. I was just thinking that between your career and your hobbies, you must meet a lot of men. Haven't you found one to marry yet?"

Her cheeks grew warm as one caustic retort after another came to mind. Intellectually, she knew Roan was only trying to get a rise out of her. He was bored, and he obviously liked to entertain himself by getting her dander up. But the emotional part of her resented his implication that she was merely fooling around with this weather stuff because it was a great way to meet men.

"I'm only trying to figure out why you chase tornadoes," he continued cheerfully.

"I have my reasons, and they're none of your business, so I'd appreciate it if you would stop speculating."

"Okay, fine," he said, unperturbed. "You ever been married?"

She threw him a murderous look.

"What? There's nothing wrong with asking that. Jeez, if we're going to be cooped up in a car for two weeks straight, I'd like to be able at least to talk to you. You know, brush up on my conversational skills."

She took a deep breath. Really, there wasn't anything wrong with the question. She was just more accustomed to Amos's less-demanding company. And perhaps she was being a bit of a poor sport because things hadn't gone exactly as she'd wished. She resolved to try to be more pleasant. "I've never been married," she said. "And before you ask why, I don't know. I've never met the right person. And you?" She intended to meet him question for question.

"Me, married? Not a chance. I never stay in one

place long enough to establish a relationship. I was raised as an army brat and I've just kept moving."

She started to argue that sometimes it didn't take all that long to fall in love, if she could believe some of the stories she'd heard. Her own parents had fallen in love on their first date and were married two weeks later. But since two weeks was the unfortunate span of time she and Roan would be together, she kept her mouth shut. With his ego, he might think she was hinting around.

"You really think we'll see a tornado today?" He leaned forward and peered at the sky through the windshield.

"I thought you didn't want to talk about weather."

"Just not all the time. But I don't see any of those cirrus clouds. Does that mean the, uh, warm, moist tongue is gone?"

Warm, moist tongue. Coming from him, that phrase didn't sound the least bit scientific.

"It's early yet," she said. "In another hour or so we'll stop and get more data."

"And lunch? You do stop for lunch, don't you?"

"I won't let you starve, but we can't indulge in a leisurely . . ." Her words trailed off as a silver Blazer, bristling with antennas, passed them going the opposite direction. She stared after the other car in her rearview mirror. "Damn," she murmured.

Roan's eyebrows sprang up. "Vicky! I didn't think you knew words like that."

She didn't bother to respond. If he wasn't going to address her by her correct name, he could just talk to the dashboard all day for all she cared.

"I mean Victoria," he corrected himself. "Sorry. But Victoria is such a long name. Four syllables. It takes a long time to say it. Vicky is quicker, more efficient, you know? Hey, what's wrong?" he asked when she didn't respond.

"That car that passed us? That was Jeff Hobbs. He works out of the Weather Service in Amarillo."

"Another chaser, I take it."

"Yeah, and a good one too, much to everyone's grief. Anytime he gets a storm that other people miss, he loves to rub it in our faces. He must have a pretty good reason for heading south. Raton would be a lot closer for him."

"You aren't thinking of changing your mind, are you?"

"Well . . . you see, Jeff is usually right."

"And you aren't?"

"Amos and I together have a pretty good track record. But by myself . . ."

"You aren't by yourself, you have me. And I say we continue north. We're halfway there already."

"That's not a good basis on which to make a decision. We could still get south in time for the show."

"Is there going to be a show? You didn't sound too optimistic an hour ago." Again he leaned forward and peered at the sky, as if it could give him the answer.

Abruptly Victoria pulled off on the shoulder, then made a U-turn in the middle of the highway.

Roan gave a hopeless sigh.

He was already getting impatient with her, she realized. But storm chasing was a lot more tedious than most people thought—hours and hours of driving, planning, figuring, consulting, and if she were really lucky, a rip-roaring, ten-minute payoff. How would Roan feel after two weeks of this?

He would probably bail out after two days. Either that, or she would get so fed up with him that she would drive back to Lubbock and dump him off.

The journey back south was quiet and tense. Victoria listened to ham radio, CB radio, an AM station out of Albuquerque, and weather radio all at the same time, trying to get a picture of how the skies were shaping up. The afternoon was getting away from them, and she still had no clear idea of where the severe weather would hit, if anywhere. Roan, alternately dozing and gazing out the window, cast a dubious look at her every so often, obviously bored and irritated by the cacophony of voices.

Toward four o'clock, Victoria saw what she was looking for—huge towers of cumulus clouds building on the horizon. She stopped the van again for gas, then pulled into a Dairy Queen.

"It's about time," Roan grumbled. But after snarfing two hamburgers, a large order of french fries, and a chocolate milk shake, his mood improved. He began to take an interest in the clouds as the van closed in on them, and even asked her to explain what the various cloud formations meant.

At five o'clock the National Weather Service issued a "T-box"—a tornado watch box—over Victoria's target area. They were still an hour away.

"Are we going to make it?" Roan asked casually.

"We'll try."

"Why don't you let me drive? I'll get us there in time."

"I'd like to get there alive, if you don't mind."

"Now, why would you—oh, I know. Unc must have warned you about my driving. All right, so when I was sixteen I smashed his pickup truck. He's been holding it against me for fifteen years."

"It's not just Amos. I saw what you did to your rental car."

"That's because I drove it off-road. I'm a good driver, really."

"How many speeding tickets have you had lately?"

"Um, how lately?"

"In the past six months?"

He fell silent. Victoria nodded, vindicated. He would touch this steering wheel over her dead body.

As they neared the town of Rhoden, the flat landscape gave way to small mountains and the clouds had formed into a definite line of storms. She picked the biggest, most well-defined one and, with Roan navigating, made use of the sparse roads to get into position ahead of it. But the storm system was not a very strong one, and disorganized at that. The winds died, the clouds broke up, and the T-box was canceled. As dusk began to fall, there was nothing left to chase.

"That's the way it goes sometimes," Victoria said, trying not to show her disappointment. It was only their first day out, after all. They would probably have plenty of chances. "Are you hungry?"

"I thought you'd never ask. No wonder you're so little. Are meals always such a low priority for you?"

Victoria was ridiculously pleased. At five foot eight, she wasn't often referred to as "little." Then again, any woman except an Amazon would be small to Roan. "If I have to choose between a hamburger and a tornado, I'll take the tornado every time," she said. "I saw one of those family-style steak houses back in Rhoden. Sound okay?"

"Yeah, sounds great. Then again, a bale of hay would sound great."

"You ate two hamburgers at four o'clock," she pointed out.

"Almost four hours ago."

She felt a small twinge of guilt. He was her guest, after all, and it wasn't very nice of her to make him uncomfortable, even if his dietary demands were a bit excessive. Tomorrow she would load up on some snacks to keep in the van.

Gus's Family Steakhouse appeared to be the social center of the town of Rhoden, and they had to wait in line. By the time they were seated, even Victoria's stomach was grumbling.

She ordered her usual from the perky waitress, a grilled chicken fillet with salad.

"I'll have a T-bone steak, medium rare," Roan said with relish when the teenage waitress batted her eyelashes in his direction. "With a baked—"

"Wait a minute," Victoria interrupted. "You can't order steak."

Roan stared at her. "Excuse me? Don't tell me you're going to make me eat health food just because you do."

"No, no, you can have anything you want except steak. You see, it's a storm-chasing tradition. We get to eat steak only if we see a tornado."

"Uh-huh."

"You can call Amos and ask him. Really."

He considered her through narrowed eyes. Suddenly his face broke into an indulgent smile. "Well, if it's that important, I guess I'll have the seafood platter."

The perplexed waitress dutifully noted his order and disappeared.

"It's silly, I know," Victoria said. "But if you want to savor the full storm-chasing experience . . ."

"Oh, I do. The full experience."

She took a long sip of her iced tea and kept her gaze averted. He was going to drive her crazy if he kept flirting with her that way.

She wasn't sure why he had such a strong effect on her. She was not an unattractive woman, and she had her share of attention from men, especially given the fact that she did, as Roan had pointed out, meet a lot of men in her line of work. But usually she found it was easy to parry suggestive remarks, ignore unwanted come-ons. She could also deliver a sizzling retort or a razor-sharp put-down if any man's comments got out of hand. But Roan's misbehavior left her tongue-tied and warm in the face.

Maybe that's because you welcome his flirtations, an impudent inner voice suggested. *Maybe you'd like to flirt right back.*

All right, so he was good-looking, a sort of modern-day Indiana Jones with a camera instead of a bullwhip.

But he wasn't her type. She wasn't sure exactly what her type was, but she couldn't possibly be compatible with someone so aggravatingly sure of his own charm. To respond to that charisma would only encourage him in the wrong direction.

Her thoughts were interrupted when someone called out her name. She looked toward the entrance to the restaurant. "Oh, no," she muttered under her breath even as she forced a smile and a wave.

"Who's that?" Roan asked.

"Jeff Hobbs. I should have known he would show up here. It's probably the only decent restaurant for a hundred miles." Please don't let him come over here, she pleaded silently. But even as she prayed, he headed through the crowded dining room toward their table, sliding his paunch between chairs.

"What are you doing here?" Jeff asked, swiveling one of the extra chairs around and straddling it. "Didn't I pass you about two o'clock heading north?"

"Mmm, possibly," Victoria hedged. She introduced the two men, who exchanged a perfunctory handshake.

"I even tried to call you a while ago on the cellular phone," Jeff continued, "to find out if you got any good video."

"Good video? Of what?" she asked crisply.

"You didn't hear?" Jeff stroked his bushy black beard, clearly relishing the prospect of breaking the news to her. "There were two tornadoes up on the Colorado–New Mexico border, near Raton. One of them was a quarter-mile wide, and stayed on the ground for almost twenty minutes."

"Raton?" she said weakly. Damn, they could have been there! "Was anyone killed?"

"Not that I've heard. I almost went that way myself," Jeff continued. "But I thought the prospects looked better down here. What made Amos change his mind?" He looked around, puzzled. "Where is Amos anyway?"

"Home sick with a cold."

Jeff nodded his understanding. She could almost hear what he was thinking: No wonder you screwed up.

"I thought it looked better down here too," she fibbed, seeking to fill the awkward silence. She wasn't willing to admit she'd followed him rather than trust her own instincts.

The waitress arrived with their dinners. Jeff looked down at the plates of chicken and seafood, clicking his tongue. "Could have been steak. Too bad."

"Yeah, well, I wasn't in the mood for beef anyway," she groused. She knew she should have invited Jeff to join them, but she didn't. He soon took the hint and, after trying unsuccessfully to extract her game plan for the following day, he left to find his own table.

Roan looked at her reprovingly, although, to his credit, he said nothing.

"I know, I know," she said. "I should have listened to you and gone with my own forecast instead of following Jeff."

"I didn't say a thing."

"But you were thinking it, and you're right. Amos is going to be disappointed in me."

Roan dipped one of his shrimp into the cocktail

sauce and popped it into his mouth. Judging from his expression, it wasn't the tastiest morsel in the world, and she regretted not letting him have his steak after starving him all day. "You don't have to tell Amos the whole story," he said.

"Yes, I do. Maybe if he gives me a good scolding, I won't be tempted to make the same mistake again."

Roan frowned. "Amos isn't your father."

But he was the closest thing she'd had to a father since she was twelve, she thought. "He's my mentor," she said. "Mentors are allowed to scold. I guess I knew someday I'd have to chase without him, but it's harder than I thought it would be."

Roan reached across the table and touched her hand. "You're doing fine. There's obviously nothing wrong with your forecasting skills—we were heading straight for Raton before you pulled that U-turn. You just need to have more faith in yourself, Victoria. We'll get 'em tomorrow, or the next day."

She heard no teasing note in his voice this time, and she saw only sincerity in those vibrant blue eyes. His hand was warm and reassuring against hers as he absently rubbed her knuckle with his callused thumb. She suppressed a pleasurable shiver that tried to wiggle down her spine.

Before she could start to enjoy herself too much, she withdrew her hand. "How's your dinner?"

He shrugged. "It'll do. I'd ask how yours is, but you haven't taken a bite."

"I will," she said, her appetite returning. She cut off a generous portion of the chicken breast and traded it to

Roan for some of his shrimp, and the meal passed with surprising cordiality. By the time she finished the slice of apple pie he'd talked her into ordering just so he could steal bites from her plate, she found she was actually liking him.

And that, she decided, was probably not wise, but there wasn't a thing she could do about it.

The shrimp tasted like they'd been frozen since the last ice age, but Roan enjoyed the meal anyway. He was glad he'd been able to offer Victoria some comfort. He was really glad she hadn't invited that creep, Jeff What's-His-Face, to join them, although perhaps in the future he shouldn't be so quick to dismiss a third party. He was relishing Victoria's solo company a bit too much.

He sat in the front seat of the parked van, twisted up like a pretzel so he could watch her in the back as she once again pulled up weather data from the computer. He'd seldom witnessed such single-minded concentration, and he was unbearably tempted to distract her—tickle the back of her neck with the end of her braid, or lean over and blow in her ear. He forced himself to resist the urge.

He knew better than to get too friendly with her. He wasn't unaware of the effect he had on women. On some women anyway. They were fascinated with his work, his thirst for adventure, his devil-may-care lifestyle. But they never stuck around long enough to really get to know him, the man inside. Or, more accurately, maybe he was the one who didn't stick around.

He wasn't a healthy influence on people who got close to him. He'd broken a few women's hearts—not intentionally, but it just seemed to happen. And then there was Kim—sweet, innocent Kim, who'd trusted him so completely. That trust had been tragically misplaced. As always, Roan swallowed back a lump in his throat when he thought about his vivacious little sister. He knew he dwelled on her, on his loss, far too much, but he couldn't seem to stop himself, especially when all these idle hours in the car gave him too much time to think.

He forced his thoughts back to his current companion, which wasn't too difficult. She occupied his mind quite a bit too.

He hardened his resolve. Best not to let pretty, proper Victoria get too fond of him—or him too fond of her. From now on, if she needed comforting or reassurance, she could find someone else to provide it. No more pep rallies courtesy of Roan Cullen. And certainly no more hand-holding. Feeling that soft skin beneath his palm, the pulse of life that beat there, had touched him at some elemental level.

As she printed up yet another map, he pretended impatience, though truthfully he was starting to find the forecasting end of storm chasing kind of interesting now that he understood the basics. And when she announced that they needed to drive north and put a couple of hundred miles behind them before seeking shelter for the night, he groaned, although he could cheerfully have ridden in the seat next to hers all night long, just watching her profile illuminated by the moon.

"Looks like Oklahoma's our best bet for tomorrow," she said as she climbed behind the wheel.

She drove tirelessly until the wee hours of the morning. Roan twice offered to drive, but she insisted she was fine. He wondered what in the hell Amos had told her. He might not hold the world's best driving record, but he certainly wouldn't take any chances with Victoria in tow.

They were in the town of Seminole, not all that far from Lubbock, their starting point, when Victoria declared they could stop for the night. She picked a motel, the Wagon Wheel, based on the fact that it featured cable TV with the Weather Channel and modular phones so she could hook up her computer modem.

She had strange priorities, Roan mused. He would have preferred someplace with a swimming pool and room service.

As they walked up to the registration desk, Roan slipped an arm around Victoria's shoulders. "Hi," he said cheerfully to the elderly female desk clerk. "I'd like the honeymoon suite for me and my new bride here."

"Roan!" Victoria jabbed him in the ribs with her elbow.

"Ouch. It was just a joke," he said as he let her go. "Woke you right up, didn't it?"

She ignored him and addressed the clerk. "We'd like two singles, on the first floor if possible."

Before long they were carrying their bags and equipment into their respective rooms, next door to each other. Victoria wasted no time turning on the Weather Channel and perching on the end of the bed to watch. Since she'd left the door open, Roan wandered in to see what was so compelling on the screen.

"Look, look, look," she said excitedly. "See that big red area all over Oklahoma? The dry line is moving east and the cold front is moving south. If any storms go up, they'll be good ones. Oh, yeah, tomorrow's the day."

He wondered if she ever got that excited about anything else—like sex. The unbidden thought brought a sudden tightness below his belt. Damn, this was no good. He was never going to last two weeks with her at this rate.

She sobered as she viewed the footage of tornado damage in Raton. "Nasty storm," she said. "At least no one was killed." She glanced over at him. "Oh, just put that down anywhere."

He realized he was still holding her tripod, which he'd carried in from the van. He set it on the floor by the window.

"Well, it's late," he said. "You're probably exhausted after all that driving, so I'll get out of your way."

She raised her arms above her head and stretched, pulling her cotton blouse tight against those firm little breasts of hers. "I'm tired, but it takes me a while to wind down from the road. Don't feel like you have to keep me company though."

He was already reaching for the doorknob. He had to get out of there. "What time . . . morning?" he asked. He couldn't articulate his thoughts with her like that, all rumpled and sleepy and looking like she needed a good tumble.

"I'd like to get on the road about ten, so we can meet around nine or so for breakfast. The restaurant next door is pretty—"

He didn't hear the rest. He was already outside, slamming the door for good measure.

FOUR

As the van carried them in air-conditioned silence toward the Oklahoma border the next morning, Roan was assailed with all manner of inappropriate thoughts concerning himself and the woman who sat a mere foot or two from him.

Today Victoria wore pale blue jeans and another proper, pressed cotton blouse, her rich russet hair neatly pinned atop her head. It was too easy for Roan to imagine what she would look like without her conservative clothes, her skin smooth and pale against scented sheets. He could feel his hands tangled in her long hair, and the warmth of her breath mingling with his. He could hear her passionate cries of ecstasy, echoing over and over in his mind. The fantasy was more vivid, more real, than any actual sex he'd ever been a part of.

And he had to stop thinking about it, dammit. She was off-limits.

"Did you say something?" Victoria asked, all innocence.

Roan realized he must have made some kind of noise in his frustration. "Just wondering how long before we get somewhere," he groused. The inactivity was getting to him. Yes, that was it. He was not accustomed to sitting in a car for hours on end. He was a physical man, always full of energy, and right now that energy was channeling itself into unwanted paths.

"We're almost into Oklahoma," she said cheerfully. Her mood was much improved from yesterday. The Weather Channel's big red splotch over central Oklahoma had still been there that morning, and all of Victoria's calculations supported the forecast for violent weather. During breakfast she'd smiled like a woman who'd just spent a lusty night with her man. That's what had gotten Roan started on his fantasies.

"Another hour or so and we'll stop," she said. "What looks like a good town?"

Roan consulted the road atlas, grateful for any distraction. "Altus isn't too far. About fifty miles, I'd say."

"Altus it is. If I recall, there's a good barbecue restaurant there."

"You mean we're actually going to stop for lunch at lunchtime?"

"Crazy, isn't it?" she said with a shrug and an easy smile. "Never let it be said I don't do something wild and impulsive once in a while."

Roan refrained from laughing out loud. That would be the day, when his Vicky did something wild and impulsive. When and if she indulged in lovemaking, she probably put it on her to-do list first.

Oh, Lord, he was doing it again. He shouldn't think about Victoria and lovemaking in the same sentence.

"Did you feel that?" she asked suddenly.

Before he could respond, the van bucked, then hesitated, then gasped a bit. "Oh, that. Yeah, I feel it."

"What's wrong with it? I'm losing power." Her voice was edged with tension. The van was indeed slowing down, and the engine was making an awful chugging noise. "Should I stop?"

Roan took a quick look around. There wasn't a speck of civilization within sight. "Not unless you like hiking through the desert."

"We wouldn't have to hike anywhere," she countered. "I can call the auto club on the cellular phone."

"And we'll be waiting into the next century for a tow. Pull over to the right lane and keep going. Maybe we can make it to the next town."

"What if I ruin the engine by driving it this way?"

"You won't," he said confidently, although actually he had no idea. "Anyway, the van is still under warranty, right?"

They had slowed to thirty miles per hour. Despite her obvious doubts, Victoria kept driving, hands clutching the steering wheel in a white-knuckled grip, her teeth tugging her lower lip. "What's the next town?"

Roan was already consulting the atlas. "Haynie. Maybe about ten miles."

"Let's hope they have a mechanic." She glanced over at Roan. "You know anything about fixing cars?"

"Yeah, but without tools and parts I can't do much." She sighed at that, and he felt an inexplicable urge to comfort her. "It's early yet. Maybe it's a minor problem, and we can get it fixed and be on our way in plenty of time to catch the storms."

"Maybe," she said without much conviction.

He couldn't blame her for her pessimism. Whatever was wrong with that engine, it didn't sound even remotely minor.

The next twenty minutes passed in tense silence as the ailing van struggled up each small incline, threatening to expire with every labored gasp of the engine. It didn't help Victoria's mood when Jeff Hobbs's silver Blazer buzzed right past them with an arrogant honk of the horn. Jerk. Didn't he notice they were having car trouble? He could have at least stopped to see if there was a problem.

At last signs of civilization began to materialize—a billboard here, a building there. "I see a gas station up ahead," Roan said.

Victoria expelled a long breath, releasing an almost palpable tension. "Thank God," she murmured.

Haynie, Oklahoma, was the epitome of a one-horse town. It sported a main street with two flashing yellow lights and one bona fide stoplight. When Victoria was forced to brake for the light, the van died and refused to start again.

"Ah, hell," Roan muttered. They were half a block from their destination, and he was going to have to push.

"Maybe they'll tow it from here," Victoria ventured to say.

Roan unfastened his seat belt. "This'll be faster. Just put it in neutral, and keep your foot off the brake."

Roan was an old hand at pushing cars. He'd once owned a Jeep that had to be push-started at least once a day. But the full-sized van was considerably heavier than a Jeep, and Roan thought he was going to have a heart attack as he heaved against the back of the vehicle with all his might. Finally it budged, never mind that they were running through the red light. It didn't matter, since there wasn't another moving car in sight. Some metropolis, this Haynie.

It seemed an eternity before he felt the van turning toward the right and into the gas station. He let up, and Victoria edged the van neatly into a parking place. Roan wiped his sweaty face with the bottom of his T-shirt as Victoria emerged from the driver's seat, looking cool and regal as always.

"Thank you, Roan," she said earnestly. "You've certainly earned your keep today."

He felt grungy and unkempt standing near her. He took a reflexive step back, away from her freshness, her springlike scent, wishing suddenly for a shower and some decent clothes. He'd never felt uneasy about his casual dress before, not for a woman, not for anyone. Lord, what was she doing to him? "No charge," he managed to say, still catching his breath.

"Something I can do for you folks?" The man who spoke was small and wizened, wearing bright red overalls over a clean work shirt. A clashing neon-green gimme cap sat atop his grizzled hair. His cheek bulged with a wad of tobacco, and as he waited for them to answer, he turned his head and spat.

Lovely. Roan felt suddenly less disgusting, by comparison.

"Our van quit," Victoria said. "We need a mechanic."

"That would be me, Leon Hornbostel at your service. Lucky for you it's a slow day. Seein' as I'm the only decent mechanic in these parts, sometimes it gets pretty backed up." He took a long, slow look at the van, then asked suspiciously, "What's all them antenneys for?"

Victoria clearly was not interested in jawing with Leon about her business. "Weather-sensing equipment," she said dismissively. "I'm with the Weather Service out of Lubbock. Before you tow the van into the garage, I need to do something. Excuse me." She climbed into the van through the side door.

Leon stuck his thumbs in his pockets and looked at Roan. "That's quite a little spitfire you got there. Wouldn't want to try to get nothin' past her, no sirree."

Roan held his hands up defensively. "She's not my spitfire. I'm just along for the ride."

Leon's eyebrows flew up, but he said nothing.

"I'm a photographer," Roan added. "I'm documenting her work."

"Is that so?" Leon glanced at the van again. "What's she doing in there?"

"Playing with her computer," Roan replied, figuring anything more technical would go right over the old man's head. "She won't be long. Got any cold drinks around here?"

"There's a machine inside the garage."

Roan found the ancient machine, bought an orange soda for an unheard of quarter, and leaned against a wall to drink it and smoke a cigarette. He'd smoked a grand total of two cigarettes the day before. At this rate, his current pack would last him the rest of the month. It wasn't that he was holding himself back around Victoria either. He simply hadn't felt much of an urge to smoke since embarking on this trip.

When he'd finished the soda and smoke, he dug a clean T-shirt with a picture of a black bear from his bag and washed his face and torso in the bathroom. As he walked back out into the hot sun, feeling much improved, Victoria emerged with a handful of printouts and her laptop computer. Roan retrieved his camera bag from the back of the van before Victoria surrendered her keys to Leon.

"If you folks want to have some lunch while I have a look-see at your engine, you can walk on down to Candy's Cafe, middle of the next block. I should have an answer for you by the time you're done eating."

"Okay," Victoria said, casting one last, distressed look at the crippled van. Rather than towing it, three young men were attempting to push it into the garage.

"It'll be all right," Roan said softly into her ear. "I checked out the garage. It's clean and neat and appears to have all the necessary tools."

Victoria nodded miserably. With her laptop clutched

against her chest, she set out in the direction of Candy's Cafe with Roan right behind.

They sat at a booth by the window. As Victoria typed rapidly on the laptop, she hardly touched the chef's salad she'd ordered. Roan showed no such concerns. He devoured his hamburger and fries with gusto, and a slice of cherry pie on top of that.

"Look at this," Victoria said more to herself than to Roan. "I've never seen such consistent, clear-cut signs. It's almost like having a giant arrow pointing right to where the tornadoes will form." Rather than sounding pleased with her findings, she sounded depressed.

"We can still get there in time," Roan said with overt optimism. He had an overwhelming urge to cheer her up. "It's only a little after noon. The van might have just thrown a belt or something. Leon might already have it fixed."

Clearly Victoria didn't buy his Little Mary Sunshine routine, so he kept quiet. She continued to fiddle with her computer, and Roan, bored and fidgety, took his camera out and checked the settings. It was a natural extension from there to snap a few shots of Victoria lost in concentration. A beam of sunshine floated in through the window, backlighting her with an unearthly halo.

He got off about three shots before she looked up.

"Stop that," she said irritably. "You're supposed to take pictures of tornadoes, not tornado chasers."

"Unfortunately, there aren't too many tornadoes in Candy's Cafe," he replied. Click. "Besides, I can't resist taking pictures of you. You look beautiful."

For a split second she flashed a smile of purely feminine pleasure, then quickly suppressed it, pinching her lips together.

"You know, Vicky, it wouldn't kill you to accept a compliment from me," he teased. "You could even smile. I promise, I wouldn't automatically take it as an invitation. I wouldn't even think of it as flirting, heaven forbid." He shot off two more frames, capturing her reaction of dismay.

"Will you cut that out?" She rolled up a sheaf of papers and thwacked him with it. "I'm glad you find me such a worthy photo subject, but you're making me nervous. I can't work."

Roan would have argued further. He was pleased he'd gotten a rise out of her. And she hadn't berated him for calling her Vicky. But they were interrupted by one of the young men from Leon's.

"Ms. Driscoll, ma'am?"

"Yes?"

"Leon says I should tell you it's your timing chain. If you'll sign this here estimate, we can order the parts from the dealership in Altus and get to work on it right away."

"Timing chain? That sounds serious. How long will it take to fix it?"

The young man laid the form on the table in front of her. "If the parts are in stock, we should have it ready by late this afternoon," he said proudly.

Victoria didn't give him the reaction he'd been looking for. She frowned, sighed noisily, then looked at the estimate. Roan read it upside down—a couple of hundred dollars plus change.

"If you had it towed to the dealership, you could get the work done under warranty," Roan pointed out.

"That would take too much time," she said. "It's okay, I can cover it." With a fatalistic shrug she signed her name to the form. The young man tipped his hat and left.

"Well, that blows any chance we had of catching up to the bad weather," she said dejectedly. "Damn, what luck. What lousy luck. This is the best-looking weather day I've seen in a long time, and we're stranded in Haynie, Oklahoma."

"Maybe we're not as stranded as we think we are," Roan offered. "I'll bet we could borrow or rent a car from someone around here, just for the afternoon."

Victoria looked hopeful for a moment before she slumped again in defeat. "No, I wouldn't want to do that."

"Why not?"

"Too risky."

"Risky how? We'll make sure the car has insurance."

"Well, of course. But we can't just take off after tornadoes in some strange car with no communications equipment."

"It'll have a radio. And we can bring the phone."

"Absolutely not." She looked down at her computer screen again, indicating the subject was closed.

Roan was intrigued with her stubbornness. What was the big deal about borrowing a car and trying to drive to where the action was? It was the kind of thing he did all the time.

"Don't you think you're being a little overcautious?" he ventured to ask.

"No."

"Well, I do. I think you rely on all your electronic gadgetry like a crutch."

"Humph." She unwrapped one of the peppermints the waitress had left with their check and popped it into her mouth.

Roan leaned across the table until his chin was almost resting on the top of the computer screen. When Victoria refused to acknowledge him, he reached around the computer and nudged her chin upward with one finger.

She looked up, her hazel eyes snapping with irritation. "What?"

"What about the romance of the sky?" he said in a provocative whisper. "What about the thrill of the chase, the challenge of facing the unknown?"

She stared at him, as if mesmerized by his voice. With their gazes locked and their mouths within inches of touching, Roan had a brief, insane notion that they might actually kiss. Then Victoria abruptly jerked away from his touch, shuttering her eyes.

"The unknown can kill people," she said curtly.

Her words had a chilling effect on Roan. He immediately backed off and did not mention borrowing a car again. She was right. When people took the elements too lightly, when they casually messed with something they knew nothing about, they could die. He better than anyone understood that.

Victoria's eyes were crossed and her fingers cramping from so much time at the laptop computer. Roan had long since grown bored. He'd paid their bill and stepped outside to smoke, much to Victoria's relief. She needed a few minutes to pull herself together.

She hadn't meant to snap at Roan. But the idea of chasing tornadoes with nothing but a phone and a radio scared the bejeezus out of her. Tornadoes weren't always visible from a distance. An HP storm—high precipitation—could be wrapped up in rain. Without the benefit of the ham radio storm spotters and the up-to-the-minute Weather Service bulletins, she and Roan could drive right into the middle of a tornado and never see the danger until their car was in the top of a tree.

She shivered at the thought, then reminded herself she had nothing to worry about. She and Roan were going nowhere without the Chasemobile, and that was final.

She couldn't really blame Roan, she thought as she closed her computer. He probably thought she was an overcautious fussbudget. But until he experienced a twister firsthand, he wouldn't understand her overriding respect toward storms, or her insistence on caution.

Even then he might not agree with her if he was as devoid of survival instinct as Amos believed.

She gave the map she'd plotted one final, longing look before folding it in half. Better to miss the action than put herself or anyone else at risk.

Roan reentered Candy's Cafe just as Victoria was

standing and stretching the kinks out of her back. "Hey, they have a pioneer museum here, in the city hall," he said in the same tone of voice he might have used to announce that he'd struck gold. "Let's check it out."

A pioneer museum? Oh, well, what else was there to do? She'd analyzed the data to death, and a little walking would do her good. Besides, his grin was infectious. "All right, you sold me," Victoria said. "But I think I'll put my computer back in the van."

That chore taken care of, they headed down Main Street to the unassuming city hall. Roan opened the door and ushered her inside.

The Pioneer Museum, in the coolness of the basement, was a hodgepodge collection of nineteenth-century farm and ranch implements, moth-eaten clothing, deeds and land grants, and samples of barbed wire. The skulls of long-dead cattle were mounted on the walls at regular intervals, staring down with hollow eyes. Sepia photographs depicted the pioneers' lives.

Fixating on the distant past wasn't high on Victoria's list of interesting things to do. She soon grew weary of the musty museum, but Roan didn't. He read every single description of every exhibit, sometimes out loud, his astute blue eyes taking in every detail.

She had to smile. His enthusiasm reminded her of a little kid, full of wonder and curiosity. While she tried to stuff her head with weather data, he seemed to have an unquenchable thirst for knowledge about everything under the sun. If there was anything pleasurable about hanging around this rusty, moldering stuff, it was watching Roan take it all in.

"You're not really liking this, are you," Roan said.

Victoria jumped. Her mind had been on her earlier calculations, and she hadn't felt Roan come up behind her. Did he have to stand so close? She could feel his breath on her hair and the heat of his body radiating toward hers.

"Uh, well . . . I guess history isn't my strongest suit," she said.

"Why didn't you say you were bored?" He immediately dragged her upstairs.

Victoria was glad to get out into the fresh air again, even if it was hot. She paused outside the city hall to study the sky. It was clear blue, with just a few flat cumulus clouds.

"Doesn't look like much of a storm day," Roan commented.

"Not here," Victoria agreed. "But a hundred and fifty miles away, those cumulus towers are already forming." She glanced at her watch, then toward the garage, tempted. New data would be available. . . .

"Oh, no you don't," Roan said, taking her by the hand and practically dragging her in the opposite direction. "You're better off not knowing what's happening a hundred and fifty miles away. You'll only torture yourself. C'mon."

She sighed and followed him meekly. He was right. She didn't really want to know what she was missing.

Next thing she knew, he ushered her into an ice cream shop called the Dairy Dilly. His hand at her waist was completely innocent, yet it sent pleasurable shivers through her body. He could be so damned appealing when he wanted to be. She hadn't missed the fact that he was trying awfully hard to keep her entertained, thus distracting her from their dismal situation.

And he was doing a pretty good job.

Victoria reveled in the air-conditioning for a few moments as she studied the Dairy Dilly's twenty-something flavors. "I'd like a small vanilla cone, please," she said decisively to the clerk.

A strangled noise came from Roan's direction. "A vanilla cone?"

"What's wrong with that?"

"You are sorely lacking in dietary imagination, Vicky." He stepped in front of her. "We'll have a triple-decker hot fudge sundae with pistachio mint, peanut-butter banana, and, ummm, mocha fudge. And two spoons." He turned triumphantly toward Victoria. "Now, doesn't that sound adventurous?"

"It sounds nauseating. And my name's Victoria." She crossed her arms and tapped her foot.

"Oops, sorry. I slipped."

"You do that a lot."

"C'mon, Vic-TOR-ee-ah," he said, enunciating her name until it sounded like it had ten syllables instead of four. "Try the sundae. If you don't like it, I'll buy you that plain ol' vanilla cone. Deal?"

She couldn't imagine why her choice of ice cream made any difference to him, but to keep the peace, she agreed. A few minutes later she found herself sitting across from him, skeptically contemplating the quivering mound of ice cream.

Roan handed her a spoon. "Dig in."

She took a small sample. It was good—very good, in fact. She took a second, larger bite, and then a third. Roan joined her, mixing all three flavors on his spoon at the same time.

"You want the cherry?" he asked.

"Do you?" she countered.

"I asked first."

"Oh, for Pete's sake, we're acting like a couple of teenagers at the malt shop. Please, eat the cherry. I won't be able to sleep tonight knowing I deprived you of it."

He laughed, dangled the fruit enticingly in front of her, then snatched it away and popped it into his own mouth, pulling it off the stem with his teeth. Victoria watched, fascinated despite herself. He had a sexy mouth.

"What's wrong with acting like kids?" he asked when he'd thoroughly chewed and swallowed the morsel. "I get the feeling maybe you've forgotten what it's like to just relax and enjoy something for its own sake, without analyzing it to death."

She narrowed her gaze. Was that really how she impressed him? An uptight scientist utterly incapable of having fun?

"I told you before, I'm very focused when it comes to a chase trip," she said, trying hard not to be offended. "If you got to know me under other circumstances, you would have a different impression of me."

"Indeed. I'd like to test that theory."

The suggestive look in his eyes left no doubt as to what "other circumstances" he had in mind. Her heart flipped over and she felt heat rushing to her face. What in the world was she to make of him? And what was she to do about her response to him? If he pressed his advantage even a little, she would melt into a whimpering pool of sexual acquiescence.

She shook her head to dispel the unwelcome images taking shape in her head, then took another bite of ice cream. A click and a whirl caused her to look up again.

"Will you stop that?" she said testily. She did not particularly want to be captured on film in her present state. She was sweaty and out of sorts, and she probably had ice cream on her nose or something just as bad.

"I like taking your picture, especially when you don't know I'm watching you. Your every thought is expressed right in your face, did you realize that?"

"I certainly hope not!" she sputtered. If that was true, she was in deep trouble.

FIVE

After the ice cream, Roan found more distractions in Haynie, Oklahoma, than Victoria had thought possible in such a dinky town. First they walked to the local high school and watched the baseball team practice. They ambled through a residential neighborhood where one of the fenced yards housed a Shetland pony, which they petted and fed handfuls of grass. Roan took more pictures. By then Victoria was getting used to it, so she didn't object.

Next they found a park, where Roan played Tarzan on the jungle gym and Victoria rocked gently to and fro on a swing, letting the breeze cool her. As he hung upside down from his knees, his T-shirt rode up, revealing rippling stomach muscles and more smooth, tanned skin than she needed to see.

When he decided to walk the highest bar like a tightrope, Victoria's pleasure turned to panic. God, he was going to break his neck. "Cut it out, Roan. You're scaring me."

He rolled his eyes, but he did climb down and came over to where she was sitting. "Want me to push you?"

"No," she answered, wary.

"Why not?"

"Because you'll push me too high, even when I tell you to slow down, and you won't stop until I scream and threaten to kill you."

He flashed a guilty grin. "You sound like you've had your share of experience with mean little boys on the playground."

"You got it." She looked at her watch. "It's after four. Let's get back to the garage and see if Leon is finished yet."

"Okay," Roan said agreeably. He'd been nothing today if not agreeable. Taking her hand and pulling her up from the swing, he said, "Now, answer truthfully. Breaking down in this little town hasn't turned out to be so god-awful bad, has it?"

She smiled. "It could have been worse. And thank you for keeping me . . . distracted. But I warn you, when I find out just exactly what we missed, my mood will go downhill in a hurry."

"Then I'll have to find some new way to, er, distract you."

The man was incorrigible, and he was getting bolder with his sexual innuendoes. But something deep inside her, something she couldn't name or explain or rationalize, let him get away with it. Perhaps it was because she suspected he wasn't serious, that he was only trying to get a reaction out of her.

Victoria already had her credit card in her hand as Leon totaled up the bill. When he gave her the charge slip, she barely even registered the amount before scrawling her normally neat signature. She was eager to check the data again.

Moments later she was staring at the computer screen and sighing. Oswego, Oklahoma. That's where the action would break, and they were three hours away. But if they hurried, they might make it.

Roan was leaning against a wall, chatting with one of the gas jockeys.

"Move it or lose it, Cullen. We've got a lot of time to make up," she called to him as she unlocked the passenger door, then walked around to the driver's side.

Roan jumped at the sound of her voice and quickly bid the other man good-bye. "Ever consider a career in the military?" he asked as he climbed into the van.

"What?"

"You've got a bit of the drill sergeant in you."

"Oh. Sorry, I didn't mean to be so abrupt. But there's a chance we'll still make it." She reached behind her and retrieved a handful of maps from the seat pocket. "Here," she said, handing them to Roan. "There's an Oklahoma map in there somewhere. Find a highway that leads to Oswego."

"Ma'am, yes, *ma'am*!"

She couldn't help but chuckle. "Cut it out."

Roan quickly plotted their shortest route to the small eastern Oklahoma town, and Victoria drove as fast as she dared. Two hours later she was encouraged by the darkening sky. The temperature outside had dropped considerably, and intermittent reports of high winds and pea-sized hail came over the ham radio. She jumped when a "beep beep beep" sounded from the weather station, followed by the announcement that the Weather Service had issued a T-box.

"All right, now we're cooking," Roan said in response to the tornado watch.

"We're still seventy-five miles away from it," Victoria said gloomily. "It'll be getting dark soon."

"Do we have to stop when it gets dark?"

"Absolutely. I don't chase what I can't see."

"Hmm." He didn't sound particularly pleased with her answer.

The ham radio spotters kept up a consistent chatter as the van approached Oswego. One reported a rotating wall cloud—the precursor to a tornado—about four miles north of town. Although visibility wasn't as good in this part of the state because of the trees, Victoria could see the supercell off in the distance. Adrenaline surged through her veins, and the air seemed to be charged with the power of the storm as the atmospheric pressure dropped.

"Find a good road north," she said, tapping the map Roan had spread out against his thigh.

"I'm looking," he said impatiently.

Another "beep beep beep" grabbed their attention. This time it was a tornado warning—a funnel cloud had been sighted.

Victoria let out a string of curses.

"Vicky!"

She turned on him. "You call me Vicky one more time and you're walking."

Roan's hurt expression made her want to bite her tongue out. "I'm sorry," he said. "I don't do it on purpose."

She eased her foot off the gas and took a deep breath. "No, I'm sorry," she said. "It's stupid for me to let the stress get to me like that. But this is very frustrating! If we just had another fifteen minutes—"

"Highway 64A," Roan interrupted. "That should be the intersection just ahead."

Victoria made a kamikaze turn onto rural route 64A, which turned out to be a twisting two-lane blacktop. "Are you sure about this?"

"It's the only decent road leading north."

Excited voices came thick and fast over the radio now, describing the tornado. According to their eyewitness accounts, the twister was long and spindly, churning across open pastures. Then abruptly the voices stopped. One man finally reported, "It's gone back up. Show's over."

"That's it," Victoria said, expelling a long breath. "It's over, and we missed it."

Sure enough, when they crested the next hill they met up with several vehicles parked haphazardly along the roadway, including TV station vans. Some of the cars she recognized as belonging to fellow storm chasers. Most were quickly packing up their video cameras and tripods, ready to zoom off to the next likely cloud in hopes of catching another storm.

She pulled up next to Eddie and Marilyn Dunne, a couple from Dallas who were amateur weather enthusiasts and regulars on the chase scene for several years.

"Victoria!" Eddie greeted her, looking surprised. "We were wondering where you'd gotten to. Jeff Hobbs said you were out and about, and I couldn't believe you weren't here. Everybody's here," he said, gesturing toward the dozen or so cars. "Did you see it?"

"I'm afraid not." She quickly introduced Roan to the couple, then asked, "What did I miss?"

"Just a little ol' rope of a storm, that's all," Marilyn said, assessing Roan with lazy green eyes. "Wasn't on the ground more than a couple of minutes. But it was kind of pretty, backlit by the sun and all. I think I got some nice stills." She patted the camera dangling from her neck.

"No damage or injuries, I hope?" That was always the first thing Victoria wanted to know about any tornado.

"No, I'm sure not," Marilyn said.

Eddie signaled for her to hurry up. "There's another wall cloud on the other side of town," he announced.

"And I suppose we're going after it," Marilyn said with a soft laugh. "You know how Eddie is. He wants to chase to the bitter end."

By that time most of the chasers were hopping into their vehicles and taking off with some urgency.

"You mean there might be another one?" Roan asked.

"Could be. These things often occur in clusters."

"Well, hell, let's go, then!"

Victoria pulled back onto the highway, working her way into the queue of cars driving like maniacs. "Shoot, we're in a lot more danger from these crazy drivers than we are from any storm," she said as someone came within inches of rear-ending the van.

"Is it always this crowded?" Roan asked.

"Lately it seems that way. Several years ago, when I first got into this business, you would never see this many chasers on the road at one time. Chasing has gotten to be a very popular pastime. I really miss the days of just me and Amos and the sky. I don't know how long it's been since we witnessed a tornado by ourselves."

"You miss him, don't you."

"Of course I do. But I must say, you've been . . . well . . ."

"A pain in the butt?"

"No, that isn't what I was going to say." What had she been going to say? That he was fun? A good sport? A helluva lot sexier than his uncle? She finally settled on "You've been quite good company." She covertly glanced in his direction to gauge his reaction.

To her surprise, a slow smile spread across his face. "You're not so bad yourself, Vic—Victoria," he said, correcting himself before he committed another nickname sin. Just when she was about to respond with a pleasant rejoinder, he added, "And you're real pretty when you're mad."

"Oh, Roan, how trite. Can't you think of anything more original?"

He just grinned maddeningly.

Even so, his silly observation sent a chill of pleasure

wiggling along her spine. Her attraction to this man was growing by leaps and bounds with every passing hour—and this was only the end of their second day together.

Victoria followed the caravan of cars, trucks, and vans as it pursued another likely-looking cloud, but her instincts told her it wouldn't pan out, and it didn't. Before long, the cacophony of voices on the radio were making dinner plans.

"Are you hungry?" Victoria asked.

"Do you even have to ask?"

"Good point. I guess we can join the others for dinner, although we'll be the only ones there not eating steak."

As they pulled into the parking lot of a little restaurant in Oswego, the cellular phone rang and Victoria answered it. "Chase II."

"Where are you?" a scratchy voice on the other end of the line asked.

"Professor! Oh, it's good to talk to you. How are you feeling?"

"Never mind me. Did you see it?"

"Um, no. We were delayed with car trouble—"

"Oh, don't tell me. You let Roan drive and he had a wreck."

"No, nothing that serious," she said. "The Chasemobile is just fine. But we missed the tornado by about ten minutes."

"Oh, I'm sorry, missy. But you'll catch one tomorrow."

"Will there be any action tomorrow?"

"Mmm, I'm not saying. It's your gig this time."

"Not even a clue?" she wheedled.

"Okay, one clue. Kansas."

"Boy, that really narrows it down."

Roan nudged her. "Let me talk to him."

"Roan wants to talk to you," she said, then handed over the phone.

"Hi, Unc. . . . Yeah, she's taking real good care of me—except for those temper tantrums. You never told me she could curse like a stevedore."

Victoria groaned and buried her face in her hands. If she survived this trip with her life, her reputation, and her heart intact, it would be a miracle.

Victoria hadn't been kidding about the steak. The storm chasers filled a long table at the restaurant, and every one of them ordered a T-bone or rib eye. The scent of all that char-broiled beef had Roan's salivary glands at full attention, and the fried chicken he'd ordered simply didn't satisfy him.

Victoria ate only a couple of bites of the pork chops she'd requested, and Roan couldn't blame her for her loss of appetite. Her so-called associates ribbed her unmercifully about her lousy luck and crummy timing, and Jeff Hobbs felt obligated to tell everyone else about her faulty decision to turn around the previous day.

It was all meant in good fun. Roan got the feeling that this was a fairly close-knit group, and everyone had endured this type of teasing at one point or another. But the fact that Victoria was a woman in an essentially male pastime seemed to add a sharper edge to the ribbing.

To her credit, Victoria handled it all with aplomb. She clearly had the ability to laugh at herself, and anyone who got too bold with his comments received a healthy dose of her acid wit. But every once in a while Roan caught a glimpse of the pain behind her tranquil hazel eyes. Her friends had no way of knowing how shaken her self-confidence was at the moment, how insecure she felt without Amos.

Eventually the talk turned to chase trips in years gone by, and Roan enjoyed hearing the war stories. As he listened to the others reminisce, he realized that each tornado had its own personality. The storms assumed a wide range of shapes, sizes, and colors. Some, like today's, were weak, short-lived, and relatively harmless. Others were destructive and deadly, causing millions of dollars in damage and loss of life.

He also began to understand something of the storm-chaser's psyche. For most of them, it wasn't just the excitement or the danger that lured them. It was more like a religion. It was something they had to do, year after year.

Roan could respect that, but he couldn't really relate to it. He was eager to experience a tornado, but once he'd accomplished that, he would be ready to move on to something else.

"Are you ready?" Victoria asked. She had leaned close so he could hear her above the boisterous chatter.

"Ready to go, you mean?" Or ready to jump on top of you? Oh, hell, he had to stop allowing these lascivious thoughts about Vicky to take him by surprise. She didn't deserve that kind of disrespect. She deserved flowers and candlelight and a man who knew how to stick around, and sticking around was one thing he didn't know how to do.

He figured it was all that moving around as an army brat. He'd learned never to form deep relationships, because that way it wouldn't be so hard to say good-bye. He was still true to his upbringing. Hadn't he just been thinking about moving on to the next thrill?

Then again, maybe Victoria herself would make a dandy next thrill.

"I'm bushed," she said, throwing some money on the table to cover their portion of the tab. Roan reached for his wallet, but she stopped him. "It's my turn. You're not obligated to finance the whole trip, you know."

Yeah, but there was enough of the macho male in him to want to buy her dinner. When the others had been teasing her, he'd had to bite his tongue to keep from defending her. And later, he'd started to feel this crazy possessiveness toward her. It was obvious the other chasers, almost all men, liked and respected her, even if they did give her a hard time. None of them were immune to her beauty either. Roan had seen quite a few covert glances in her direction, eyes full of admiration and sometimes downright lust. And he'd felt good knowing that later he would leave with her, and have her all to himself—at least for as long as it took them to find a motel and book separate rooms.

He sighed at the hopelessness of the situation. It was

hell being attracted to a woman who was strictly off-limits.

As they left the restaurant, the cool evening air surprised them. Victoria shivered. "Brrr, the cold front is definitely here."

In a purely reflexive gesture, Roan slid an arm around her shoulders and rubbed her bare arm. Amazingly, she didn't resist, didn't even act surprised. She just tucked herself against his shoulder as they walked briskly across the parking lot. He supposed that meant she'd come to trust him—which made him feel doubly guilty for the things he was thinking about her.

She fumbled with the keys in her purse. Roan took them from her and unlocked her door as he sheltered her from the keen wind with his body. But instead of opening the door, he pressed the keys into her hand, then swiveled her around so she was facing him, her back against the van.

"You are one helluva woman, you know that?"

"Wh-what are you talking about?"

"Back there in the restaurant. When those yo-yos were giving you such a hard time. Most women would have dissolved into tears after the first thirty seconds. But you took it all with perfect grace, and you gave as good as you got."

"Oh, them." She waved her hand dismissively. "They don't bother me." Her voice trembled slightly—whether from emotion, the cold, or the fact that Roan was standing far too close to her, he could only guess.

"I think they did bother you. But we'll show 'em,

Vic. We'll be in plenty of time for the next tornado. We'll get there hours ahead of anyone else, even if we have to get up at six in the morning to do it."

"Vic?" she repeated, ignoring the rest of his pep talk.

"Well, you didn't like Vicky."

"And I don't like—" He cut her off with a kiss. He'd meant only to peck her on the lips to halt her argument, but somehow his plan didn't take shape quite like that. Before he knew what was happening, his mouth was pressed against hers as he savored the sweet taste of her. He grasped her shoulders, pulling her against him until he could feel the gentle push of her small, rounded breasts against his chest. He even fancied he could feel the dark heat of her womanliness radiating outward, encompassing him, pulling him deeper and deeper.

She didn't resist when he probed her mouth with his tongue, and she even met his forays with tentative flicks of her own tongue. She might as well have doused him with gasoline and thrown a match at him. No subtle act of acceptance had ever turned him on so quickly, so thoroughly, so . . . uncontrollably.

"Victoria," he murmured against her lips. He'd always had trouble with her name, but now it resounded like poetry in his mind, beautiful and dignified and secretly hot, like the woman herself.

He kissed her ear, her neck, her throat. She clutched his shoulders in a painfully tight grasp, but she didn't push him away. Carried by the heat of the moment, he undid two buttons on her blouse and dipped his tongue between her breasts. Her skin smelled like delicate wildflowers, sweet and clean and exotic all at the same time.

She insinuated her thigh against his arousal, exerting a gentle, excruciating, and quite deliberate pressure. Overcome, he plunged his hands inside her blouse and covered her breasts, kneading them beneath her lacy bra.

"Uh, Roan . . ." She could barely utter the words, she was breathing so hard.

God help him, he wanted her so badly, he could have taken her right there in the dark parking lot.

"Please . . ."

That single word, spoken with so much desperation, brought him back to his senses. This was crazy! Though it almost caused him physical pain, he slowly pulled away. Moonlight revealed the play of emotions on her face—desire, confusion, dismay.

She clutched the front of her gaping blouse, glancing guiltily over his shoulder. "Someone could see us."

"Then let's go somewhere more private."

"No!" There was a definite edge of panic in her voice. "Look, Roan, I promise not to whine about our bad luck anymore if you promise not to . . . comfort me."

"Comfort you?" he repeated. "If you think I had comfort on my mind just now, you must not have much experience with men and their . . . hormones."

His were still raging.

She bristled at that. "I have as much experience as I need, thank you. Don't feel obligated to educate me. Now, can we please get in the car?"

He released her. He would let her think she'd won this round—for a minute or two anyway. However, as soon as they were in the van, seat belts dutifully buckled, he asked, "Are you a virgin?"

She made an exasperated noise. "Roan, please, I don't want to talk about this. You shouldn't have kissed me."

"And you shouldn't have kissed me back."

That silenced her for a moment. "Point well taken." She said nothing for a long while, and he didn't pursue it. When she spoke again, she took him by surprise. "I'm thirty years old. Of course I'm not a virgin."

He chuckled, and the tension between them ebbed slightly. *A little defensive, Vicky?* He knew she wasn't totally lacking in experience. No woman with that kind of fire could ignore the pull of her own sexuality for too long. But he wondered if any man had ever fully explored her depths and kindled that fire into a raging inferno. He'd like to. He'd really like to.

"Amos would kill you," she said, almost as if she'd read his thoughts.

"Yeah, I know," he agreed reluctantly.

"And I don't intend to be your two-week fling, have you got that?"

"Loud and clear." When he really thought about it, he couldn't imagine Victoria being anyone's fling. Flings were intended to be enjoyed and forgotten, and she was simply not a forgettable woman.

SIX

Victoria let the lukewarm shower spray prod her out of her morning grogginess. She hadn't slept well, what with unfulfilled urges humming through her body and self-recriminations echoing in her restless mind. She'd hoped that what she and Roan had done the night before wouldn't seem so awful by morning's light.

But it did.

She was mortified that she had let herself get so carried away. Whatever Roan had intended with his kiss, she'd been looking for comfort. He was the only one who understood what she'd been through the past two days, and after the brutal teasing she'd been subjected to, she'd felt a peculiar kinship with him. He hadn't criticized or condemned or complained. And during that one weak moment, when he'd captured her lips with his, she'd wanted to dissolve in that solace.

And something else. Ever since she'd met Roan she'd sensed that something more serious lay beneath his brash, irreverent exterior. As their lips met and their breaths mingled, she'd felt an odd sensation of brushing up against the real Roan, a man of depth and complexity and, yes, even tragedy.

Within seconds, all ordered thought had vanished as her body came alive. Swept into a maelstrom of pure sensation, she'd dismissed all thoughts of what was proper or prudent. Somehow, perhaps because of the overwhelming nature of the kiss, she'd realized that Roan was no safe haven, but the embodiment of danger itself. She'd dug deep into herself and found the presence of mind to issue a small protest.

To his credit, he'd responded immediately, releasing her, allowing her to pull away. She'd grabbed on to that concession with both hands, letting anger set in. It wasn't exactly fair to be angry with Roan. He hadn't done anything so terribly wrong. But the harsh words had served their purpose—to erect a strong, impenetrable barrier between them so that nothing like that would happen again.

The situation wasn't hopeless, she decided. Roan had charmed her into letting her guard down, that was all. The wisest course of action would be to retreat to a more formal relationship. With that decision made, she felt slightly better.

She shivered as she stepped out of the shower and vigorously began drying herself. After pulling on white jeans and a thin lilac sweater, she plopped down on the end of the bed, turned on the Weather Channel, and began the laborious task of combing the tangles out of her long hair.

The forecast surprised her. She had really thought the past two days of violent weather would be the last she would see for a while; only so much atmospheric energy was available for a storm to draw on. But it appeared the storms weren't completely played out. The map showed a red splotch over Kansas, indicating potential for tornadic activity.

"Ha!" she said aloud, turning on her laptop computer. Amos had been right about Kansas. She pulled up the latest data, made some calculations, colored a new map, then picked up the phone and dialed Roan's room number. This was one show she wasn't going to be late for.

"Hmph?" Roan answered. The sound of his sleep-scratchy voice brought an unexpected tightness to her chest. There was something so damnably intimate about talking to a man when he was in bed, even if it was over the phone. What did he sleep in? she wondered.

"Good morning, Roan," she said crisply.

"Oh, mornin', Vic," he said, his voice filled with warmth.

She decided to ignore his new title for her. He was, after all, still half asleep. "Sorry to wake you, but I'd like to get on the road early today. We may have one more shot at a tornado, and I don't want to take any chances of getting there late."

"Sure, okay. How'd you sleep?"

"I slept fine," she lied, taken aback by the question. Roan wasn't normally concerned with her sleeping habits. "And you?"

"Not too good. Kept dreaming about big hazel eyes

shining in the moonlight, and the softest lips this side of—"

"I'm so sorry," she cut in. "Perhaps we can stop at a drugstore and buy some Ny-tol. That should help get rid of those annoying dreams."

Silence greeted her clinical, unemotional response—precisely as she'd intended. She would not answer in kind when he flirted with her, and she would not get angry either. Those were the two reactions he aimed for. If she did not provide them, he would stop provoking her.

"Well, uh . . ." he finally managed to get out.

"Can you meet me in the motel restaurant in about thirty minutes?" she asked smoothly.

"Yeah, sure."

"All right. See you then." She hung up, feeling deflated. But it was good to know her plan was working.

Breakfast was a grim affair. Like Eliza Doolittle at the horse races, Victoria restricted her conversation to health and weather—mostly weather. Roan demolished a Denver omelet, offering only a nod or a monosyllabic answer when she asked him a direct question. But she was constantly aware of the way he watched her, almost as if he were sizing her up for his next meal, and she couldn't help the breathless catches that sometimes punctuated her words, or the blood that rushed to her face and then abruptly away, leaving her light-headed.

Wondering how he would kiss had been bad enough. Now that she knew, his effect on her was twice as devastating. Why did he have to be so all-fired . . . masculine?

After the meal Roan seemed to come to a decision. Victoria could almost see his chin tensing with resolve as he paid their bill. His blue eyes glinted with a new determination. Or was she only being fanciful?

No, he was definitely up to something, she decided when, as they were loading their gear into the van, he lit a cigarette right in front of her. Until that point he had considerately restricted his smoking to times they were apart.

She closed the back doors of the van and turned, only to find herself practically chest to chest with him. "So you're just going to ignore what happened last night, is that it?" he asked. The question was issued amiably enough, but there was an edge to his smile.

"That was my general plan, yes," she said, trying to sidle away from him. She couldn't think when he was so close.

He placed both hands against the van on either side of her, effectively trapping her. "Unh-unh. Stay here and talk to me. Was that one kiss so earth-shatteringly awful?"

"No, of course not. It was a very nice kiss, as kisses go." *Understatement of the year.* "But it was unwise, and you know that as well as I do."

"So you want to ignore it?"

"Yes, very much."

"Does that mean you want to ignore me as well?"

"I haven't been ignoring you."

"Not ignoring me, exactly. Freezing me out is more like it." He flicked away the half-smoked cigarette. "You and I, we had a rough start. But I thought we were beginning to get along. I thought we were starting to understand each other. I thought . . . ah, hell, what am I doing?" He pushed himself away from the van, away from her, looking completely disgusted. He walked over to the smoldering cigarette he'd discarded and stomped on it with far more force than necessary, practically grinding it into dust. "You ready to leave?"

Guilt nagged at Victoria's conscience. Her behavior had been intended to protect herself, to put a barrier between them. But she hadn't intended to hurt Roan's feelings, which was apparently what she'd done. It had never occurred to her that rough-and-tumble Roan Cullen would have the sensitivity to be stung by her coldness.

All right, so maybe her perception of him was lacking. Before she'd met him, she'd painted him in her mind as a macho hotshot, and much of what she'd seen during their first meeting had reinforced that impression. But she ought to know by now that there was more to him. She'd seen glimpses of compassion, especially the previous day, when he'd worked so hard to keep her entertained while the van was in the shop.

He didn't deserve what she'd given him this morning. "Roan . . ."

But he'd already walked away, climbed into the passenger seat and slammed the door. Determined, she opened her door and slid in beside him, but she didn't start the engine. "Look, I'm sorry, okay? But I had to put some distance between us. Keeping things on a more formal, less personal level seems like a good idea."

"You could just say, 'Roan, don't kiss me again.' That would work."

No, it wouldn't, she argued silently. Because next time she might have been the one to kiss him. The distance had been for her benefit as well as his.

"Yeah, well, never mind," he said. "Let's just get on the road and forget this whole stupid discussion."

"No, I can't forget about it. I've obviously hurt your feelings, and I never meant—"

"You didn't 'hurt my feelings,' for God's sake," he interrupted, throwing his hands in the air. She should have guessed he wouldn't admit to anything as unmanly as emotions. "I just don't fancy spending the next week and five days with an iceberg."

"An iceberg!" she sputtered. But when she stopped and thought about it, that was a pretty apt description of her demeanor. "Well, better an iceberg than a raging forest fire." She hadn't realized she spoke her last sentiment out loud until she looked at Roan and saw the hardness in his face soften to gentleness tinged with amusement.

"You mean with a little effort I could turn you into a raging—"

"No, that's not what I meant," she retorted, leaning her forehead against the steering wheel. But her face, at any rate, was certainly flaming.

Roan's long, hearty laugh sounded like it came from somewhere deep within him. Although Victoria should have been incensed that he would be amused at her expense, somehow she couldn't find any more anger inside herself. That laugh was a terrific ice breaker, and she actually smiled at the absurdity of the whole situation. She leaned back and folded her arms, waiting to see what he would say or do next.

When his laughter died down, he offered her a new proposition. "Okay, Vic—Victoria," he said. "I think I understand your position a little better now. And I agree that any, er, physical involvement between us would be dumb. So how about this: If I promise to be a perfect gentleman for the rest of this trip, will you stop treating me like I have leprosy?"

Victoria made an unladylike snort. Then a giggle escaped, and finally a full-blown burst of laughter. "You, a perfect gentleman? On what planet?"

"Hey, with the exception of one or two minor lapses, I've done okay so far. C'mon, Vic, be a sport. I'm offering to curb my baser instincts, and all you have to do is be nice to me. I'd say you have the easier task. I'm easy to be nice to." He extended his hand to her. "Deal?"

"Golly, how could I say no?" She gingerly shook his hand, and he smiled at her, a devilish glint in his gaze. Somehow, she got the feeling that Roan would be hard-pressed to remain a "perfect gentleman" for twelve minutes, let alone twelve days.

Given the day's disastrous start, the drive up into Kansas went relatively smoothly, Roan thought. Despite the tongue-in-cheek manner in which he and Victoria had made their "deal," he was determined to honor his promise to her. He kept his flirtations on a strictly surface level, and even made every attempt to use her full name, although "Vic" slipped out of his mouth more often than not.

To her credit, she'd stopped snapping at him every time he transgressed. In fact, she seemed warmer and more human than he'd ever seen her. He liked it. He liked it a lot.

Ah, hell, he liked it too much. She was getting under his skin in a big way. Everything about her turned him on, from the slope of her cheek to her dainty, long-fingered hands, to her long, denim-clad legs. Even her voice, so soft and feminine, tickled his senses like a feather.

He hadn't wanted to admit it, but her coldness that morning had cut him to the quick. He'd thought she was acting that way out of some misguided desire to punish him for the perfectly natural urge he'd followed to kiss her. It was only after she'd made that "raging forest fire" comment under her breath that he realized her behavior had been a natural self-protective instinct. Immediately he'd felt different about everything.

He was glad they'd talked things out. He was not particularly looking forward to spending countless days with her, unable to touch her. But that's how the chips had fallen.

It was better that way, he reminded himself again and again. She wasn't the type of woman for a casual fling, and he wasn't the type of man to offer anything more. Permanence wasn't in his vocabulary. Even if he'd wanted it—which he didn't, he told himself firmly—he didn't believe he was capable.

"I'd always heard Kansas was flat," Roan remarked as they traveled along a rural highway with acres and acres of newly greening wheat fields stretching out in all directions as far as the eye could see. "They weren't kidding. It's even flatter than Oklahoma."

"Great tornado-chasing country," Victoria said. "How far are we from the target area?"

"About forty miles, close as I can estimate," Roan said. There hadn't been a sign or a mile marker in quite a while.

"Close enough. We're early, for once."

Roan scanned the horizon. "These clouds don't look too menacing."

"Just wait. Pretty soon those innocent-looking, puffy little clouds will start building higher and higher—if the cap isn't too strong—and we'll have ourselves a dandy tornado. Mark my words."

He didn't know what she meant by "the cap." He decided not to ask. He'd had enough meteorology education for a lifetime. "Quite the little optimist today, aren't you?"

"Hey, the signs look good. What's the town we're heading for? Oh, yeah, Barricklow. We can stop there, gas up, grab some lunch—"

"And check the data again." He knew the routine by heart.

Barricklow, Kansas, wasn't quite as small as it looked on the map. It featured a real downtown area, complete with an old movie theater, a radio station, and a chain department store. Victoria drove aimlessly along the quaint streets until she found a likely-looking cafe for lunch.

"You don't like fast food," Roan said.

She wrinkled her nose. "I try to watch my diet when I'm on these trips. We don't get very much exercise."

Immediately Roan thought of a dozen ways he and Victoria could burn off a few calories, all of them X-rated.

"We can go someplace else if you'd rather," she offered, misinterpreting his moment of contemplation for hesitation about her choice of restaurant.

"Oh, no, this is fine." He opened the door and ushered her in ahead of him, forcing his gaze and his thoughts away from her delectable body. If he was going to survive this trip, he needed to give his mind something to focus on besides Victoria Driscoll.

Engine parts. Anytime he felt his willpower ebbing, he would mentally take apart the engine of the old Ford LTD he used to own. Didn't prisoners in solitary confinement do that to keep from going crazy?

After they'd browsed the stained, dog-eared menus and made their selections, Victoria got downright chatty. She asked him all sorts of questions about his childhood, his education, his work. He actually found the conversation pleasant, since it kept his mind off other, more forbidden subjects. Was it possible he and Victoria were becoming . . . friends?

When their sandwiches arrived, he turned the tables on Victoria, asking her about her childhood, her friends, her garden, her job at the Weather Service, how she got hooked up with Amos. And she answered obligingly, much more open about herself now that the parameters of their relationship had been established.

Only one of his questions produced any hesitation, and that was when he asked her about her father.

"He died when I was twelve, very suddenly," she replied in clipped tones. "Fortunately, he left my mother and me very well provided for." And that was all she offered.

Sensing the subject was somehow tender for her, he didn't push—just as she didn't push when he made a similarly brief mention of his younger sister's death. They were starting to trust each other, but that trust stretched only so far.

As she paid their bill at the cash register, Roan noticed an advertisement for a bungee-jumping attraction. "Hey, look at this," he said, pointing out the flyer in the window to Victoria.

"Hmm?" she said distractedly, still stuffing her change into her purse.

"Bungee jumping. Ever tried it?"

Her eyes widened. "Certainly not. And I suppose you have?"

"Actually, no. I've always thought it sounded like fun, but I never really had the opportunity. Want to go take a look?"

She appeared horrified. "Absolutely not. Bungee jumping"—and she said it with a delicate curl of her upper lip—"isn't on our agenda."

"But you said yourself that we have hours to spare, and we're smack in the middle of the target area. If we have time to kill—"

She shook her head vehemently. "No, thanks. Time to kill doesn't mean time to kill ourselves."

"Okay, then, how about if I hitch out there while you do your computer thing, and then you can pick me up on your way out of town."

Now she seemed downright agitated. "No, really, Roan, I don't think you should. You could break your neck."

"Aw, come on, you sound like my mother."

"Well, I'm sorry, but it *is* dangerous. I saw this piece on that home video TV show where the rope broke and this guy was paralyzed—"

"The rope won't break. That's a one-in-a-million occurrence."

She pursed her lips and looked down at her feet.

The diner's cashier, a middle-aged woman with a mountain of dyed black hair atop her head and painted-on eyebrows, chose that moment to interrupt. "Say, if you're thinking about that bungee-jumping thing, I'd highly recommend it," she said. "I did it yesterday—biggest thrill of my life, I'm telling you. My kid did it twice. And some of the profits are going toward the Lion's Club summer camp program, so it's for a good cause."

"See there?" Roan said. "What do you think?"

"I can't stop you from doing it, if that's really what you want to do," Victoria said quietly. "But I don't see the point in risking your life merely for the sake of a thrill. I just . . . wish you wouldn't, that's all."

God, her lower lip was trembling. Did the thought of him breaking his neck really upset her that much?

"Okay, I won't do it," he said. "But let's at least go out there and watch. I'd love to get some pictures. And frankly, if this tornado thing doesn't pan out into some decent video footage, I need to make this two weeks count for something in the bank."

Once he'd capitulated, she immediately softened. "Okay, we'll go watch."

They went back to the van so Victoria could go through her by-now-familiar data-pulling process. She didn't spend as much time as she usually did, declaring after only a cursory inspection of the information that little had changed since the morning. All systems were go. They would drive north of town, find the highest vantage point, and wait to see what the clouds would do.

"The bungee-jumping platform would be a pretty high vantage point," he said.

She sighed. "All right, all right, we'll go watch a bunch of fools participating in a suicidal activity," she said. "But I don't see what's so amusing about it."

They found the bungee-jumping outfit in a huge discount-store parking lot on the edge of town. The platform was so high that the people on it looked no bigger than ants. On the ground below them was a huge expanse of some type of cushioning device.

As Roan was pulling his camera bag out of the back of the van, a jumper made the plunge. Victoria let out a little squeak of distress, followed by a sigh of relief. "Oh, thank goodness, he's not hurt."

"Victoria, very few people have been injured on these things. They wouldn't keep doing it if it weren't relatively safe. Hell, it's probably safer than driving on the highway."

"I don't know about that," she said, shaking her head.

They moved in closer. "My gosh, parents have brought their children here," she said in amazement. "Would you ever let your child do this?"

"I don't know. I don't have any children."

"Well, I can tell you, no child of mine would get within a hundred feet of this thing." Before the words were even out of her mouth, a youngster of about twelve approached them, staring in awe at Roan's display of photographic equipment. "You from the newspaper?"

"No, just a freelance photographer. Have you done this before?" Roan asked, nodding toward the platform.

"Oh, sure, twice already. I spent all last summer's grass-mowing money, and it was worth every penny."

Roan smiled. "Tell her what it's like," he said, looking at Victoria.

The boy focused his attention on her. "Oh, lady, you should give it a try. It's like flying. And it's not dangerous or anything, because my mom wouldn't let me do it if it was. Heck, she's gonna try it tomorrow when she's off work."

At that moment another body took a nosedive from the platform, careening toward earth at a heart-stopping speed, then stopped gently as the huge elastic cable checked the fall. Roan snapped off several shots. The woman on the end of the line, squealing delightedly, had to be at least sixty. Maybe he could sell a feature shot to one of those magazines for senior citizens.

"Oh, my God, look at that old woman!" Victoria said. "What if she had a heart attack?"

The boy, still hanging around, clapped his hands and whistled through his teeth. "Way to go, Granny," he said. Then he turned back to Victoria and Roan. "That's my grandmother. And she doesn't have a heart condition. They won't let anybody jump who's sick or feeble or anything. They got strict rules, you know?"

Roan smiled smugly at Victoria, who merely looked bewildered.

Roan approached the woman who'd just finished her jump and asked her if she would provide some information about herself and sign a model's release form. Still breathing rapidly from the excitement, she was happy to oblige.

Victoria came up beside them. "Excuse me, but weren't you scared to death?"

"Oh, my, yes, of course I was scared," the older woman said, laughing. "That's the whole point, don't you think? But it was like landing in a mountain of feathers. Not a scratch on me, not even a strained muscle. Just a sore throat from screaming. You should try it, honey."

"But how can you be sure it's safe?" Victoria persisted.

"Ain't nothin' a hundred percent safe," the woman said. "But if you're really worried, there's an inspection certificate by the ticket booth. The whole setup is looked over by an engineer at least once a day. Why, if you just look at the thing yourself, you can tell it's sturdy. I bet a hundred people have jumped today alone, and not a one's had a single complaint."

Victoria stuck her thumbs in her pockets, gazing pensively at the scaffolding that supported the platform.

Roan had promised her he wouldn't jump, and he couldn't change his mind now, or she would never trust him again. But if she changed her mind about it first . . .

"You know," she said slowly, thoughtfully, "maybe this thing's not so crazy after all."

Yes! he said silently.

"If a twelve-year-old kid and a grandmother can do it with hardly a blink, it couldn't be all that bad. And it's inspected by an engineer. . . ."

"Then you don't mind if I give it a whirl?" he ventured to ask. "It's up to you. If you really don't want me to, I won't."

"Well, actually . . . I was thinking maybe I would try it."

"What?"

"Well, why not? Aside from chasing tornadoes, which really isn't all that dangerous, I've never done anything very exciting. I'll bet Amos would get a kick out of hearing about—"

Roan couldn't describe the horror he felt at the realization that he'd convinced Victoria Driscoll to do something so crazy. She was an intelligent, cautious woman, and after spending a couple of days with him she was talking about plunging hundreds of feet with nothing to protect her but a rubber band. Was he that rotten an influence?

Abruptly he looked at his watch. "I don't think we have time," he said, suddenly all business. "That waiting line at the bottom of the platform is pretty long, and we don't want to miss those tornadoes. I have enough shots of this." He started packing up his cameras and lenses.

"But, Roan . . ."

"Anyway, it doesn't look like that much fun. And did you see how much it costs? Thirty bucks for thirty seconds worth of terror. Big deal." He practically dragged her back to the van and stuffed her in.

As soon as they were on the road again, he allowed himself a sigh of relief.

"I don't get it," Victoria said, shaking her head. "One minute you're itching to try bungee jumping, and the next you're convinced it's all a big bore. What gives?"

"Nothing gives. It's just that, after watching it for a few minutes, I decided it didn't look all that great." And he would not, could not be responsible for causing another human being to take a risk with her life, even a small one. Accidents did happen. People had been killed bungee jumping. If anything were to happen to Victoria . . .

He'd already caused the death of one innocent young woman. And not just any woman, but one whose safety he'd sworn to protect. After it was all over and the numbness had worn off, he'd barely found the will to live. And sometimes, when he lay in his bed in the dark of night, he still wished he'd died instead of her.

As Victoria concentrated on her driving, Roan studied her at leisure. Friends? That was pure delusion. He felt far more than mere friendship for Victoria Driscoll. What a tragedy that he was so utterly wrong for her.

There were all sorts of reasons she was beyond his reach. For one, Amos would freak if Roan took advantage of the situation. And two, he could not possibly give Victoria the time and attention she deserved beyond the next twelve days. As soon as this trip was over, he was scheduled to travel to Switzerland to make a documentary on the Olympic training program there, and maybe get in some skiing. From there it was on to Guatemala, where they were digging up a Mayan city, and then, who could tell?

If he were honest with himself, though, all of Uncle Amos's objections, and all of the logistical problems in the world couldn't have stopped him from pursuing Victoria. Not even his promise to behave himself would hold him back for long.

But one thing stopped him cold. He knew beyond a doubt that if she were to fall in love with him, he would hurt her. There was a good chance he would get himself killed one of these days. He had no intention of leaving behind a grieving lover.

SEVEN

Victoria puzzled for some time about Roan's peculiar behavior. If she hadn't known better, she would have thought he'd chickened out of bungee jumping at the last minute. But she couldn't imagine that Roan Cullen, a man who had faced hurricanes and volcanoes, a man who'd almost gone over Niagara Falls in a barrel, could be afraid of anything, much less something as relatively tame as jumping off a platform attached to a giant rubber band.

But she'd seen something in his eyes, something she could easily interpret as fear, even panic.

After a while, however, she consciously dismissed the incident from her mind. What business was it of hers if he'd changed his mind about bungee jumping? Anyway, the weather needed her full attention.

The expected focal point of violent storms had moved north and east. Victoria headed for a small hill—more of a rise, really, since they were in central

Kansas. But it afforded them a good vantage point from which to watch the sky. She pulled off the highway, cut the engine, and opened her door, grateful for the warming temperature.

Roan followed her example, but he had nothing to say. He lit another cigarette, took a couple of drags, made a face, and threw the rest away.

"I don't believe I've seen you finish a cigarette since we started this trip," she commented as she donned a baseball cap to shield her eyes from the sun.

"They haven't really tasted good lately," he said with a shrug. And then he wandered away to fiddle with his camera equipment. Victoria got the distinct impression he wasn't in a chatty mood, and so she kept quiet herself. One of the things Amos had always praised her about was her ability to enjoy a period of quiet, and not constantly try to fill silence with inane conversation.

But all the same, she had to bite her tongue to keep from asking Roan what was on his mind.

Victoria forced herself to concentrate on the magnificent view, allowing the warm sun and the breeze to wash away her tension. Because of the flatness of the land, she could see for miles in every direction. The gently undulating fields formed an endless palate of greens, yellows, and browns, dotted with an occasional white farmhouse. The understated beauty of this countryside apparently wasn't lost on Roan. He was framing shots with his camera, trying out different lenses and filters. His results might not be the sort of dramatic nature shots found in *National Geographic*, but if he could capture the subtleties of light and color . . .

Victoria's gaze strayed far too often in Roan's direction. She couldn't deny he was easy on her eyes, more interesting than the drifting clouds and lengthening afternoon shadows. Unaware of her scrutiny, he moved with the grace and agility of a natural athlete, sometimes dropping to one knee to steady his shot, or just gazing at the horizon, his expression reflecting an inner turmoil Victoria couldn't begin to understand.

Her heart ached for him, and she didn't even know why. Her body ached for him, too, in a much more insistent way. Now *that* needed no explanation. She still couldn't get his kiss completely off her mind. She recalled in exquisite detail the insistence of his mouth against hers, the feel of his warm, sure hands seeking out her softness.

Her body reacted as if the kiss were more than a memory, and she made a heroic effort to turn her thoughts elsewhere. It served no purpose to fantasize about Roan. She'd made her decision not to get involved with him, and she was sticking by it. She had no hope of understanding the man. She had no chance of controlling his self-destructive behavior, despite Amos's hopes. And she had never felt comfortable around things she couldn't understand and control—at least to some degree. Life offered too many risks already without a person looking for them.

Victoria scanned the sky and smiled with self-satisfaction. The clouds were cooperating nicely, churning and merging and building into huge cumulus towers that seemed to reach into infinity. An occasional flash of lightning could be seen in the distance. Her forecast couldn't have been more accurate.

She liked one storm in particular, which was forming all by itself without any neighbors to suck away its energy, and she kept a careful eye on it.

Roan, too, was watching it, she noticed. "What do you think of that one?" he asked with a degree of enthusiasm she hadn't heard since they'd left Barricklow.

"It's promising," she replied. "See how the tops of the clouds have nice, crisp edges? And how they look kind of like cauliflower florets? That's a good sign. As a matter of fact, we ought to get in the van and get closer to it."

"Let's do it." Roan stowed his gear in the back of the van, then climbed into the passenger seat. His step had seemed a little quicker, his gestures more animated. Victoria was hopeful that he'd forgotten whatever had made him so preoccupied earlier. She didn't like to see him so serious.

Funny, when she'd first met him, she'd have given anything to see him a little more serious. But now, of all things, she missed his teasing. He'd been keeping his promise about being a gentleman—keeping it too well.

She pulled the Kansas map out from behind her seat and handed it to Roan. "I'd like to position ourselves north and east of the storm, so it's coming toward us."

"You want it to chase us instead of the other way around?"

"Exactly. There's more to see in front of a storm than behind it. But don't worry. As long as we know what direction it's traveling, we can get out of the way."

"I wasn't worried," he said with a crooked grin. "How far are we from the action?"

"I'd say about ten, maybe fifteen miles."

He consulted the map. "Let's see . . . there should be a turnoff to the right for K-22 a couple of miles farther. Then, if we take this YY road . . . yeah, that should work."

"What kind of a road is YY?" Victoria asked.

"Solid black line. Turns into a dotted line farther north, but I don't think we'll be going that far."

"Does it have some cross streets? I don't like to get myself cornered."

"Mmm, not many. The roads are pretty few and far between out here."

She had to agree with him. The wide-open spaces of the rural Midwest made for great visibility, but that same emptiness meant sparse roads. She'd lost more than one promising storm out there when it went one direction and the road went another. And she liked to keep her options open.

Well, they'd just have to do the best they could.

When they turned off onto K-22, Victoria saw that she was not the only chaser on the trail of this particular storm. A van from a Wichita television station was up ahead of her. And within moments she saw Jeff Hobbs's Blazer behind her.

"Looks like we're not alone," Roan observed.

"I didn't figure we would be," Victoria said wistfully. "Any yo-yo watching the Weather Channel knew enough to be in the vicinity. And once here, there was no question about which storm to watch. This one's going to be a dilly."

In the last few minutes as they'd neared the storm, the skies had grown progressively darker. Victoria switched on the video camera mounted on the dashboard. Excited voices flew thick and fast over the ham radio as spotters reported the location of the storm cell, the velocity and direction of its movement, and the pea-sized hail falling in its wake.

Victoria herself could see that the storm in question churned violently. An ominous lowering looked suspiciously as if it were rotating, and Victoria's every instinct told her they were about to see the birth of a tornado.

"I need a road north," she said, trying to keep her nerves under wraps. This was the real test. Could she keep cool during this kind of stress without Amos's calming presence? She'd never witnessed a tornado without her able mentor by her side.

"YY," Roan said, equally calm but with an underlying excitement in his voice. "It's coming up. See where the TV van is turning?"

"Oh, right. YY. You told me that before, didn't you."

Roan was too busy staring out the window at the wall cloud to answer. He was obviously transfixed by the awesome sight. "It's gonna happen." He barely breathed the words.

"I think it is. This many chasers couldn't be wrong." Finding a parking space along the roadside proved to be a challenge, but Victoria finally wedged the van between two crookedly parked cars. Wasting no time, she unfastened the video camera, grabbed a tripod from the floor behind her seat, and jumped out of the van. Following her cue, Roan was making similar preparations. In fact, everywhere she looked, people were scurrying around trying to get cameras set up. The man from the TV station was attempting to find someone to interview while his camerawoman filmed the storm, but there were no takers. Everyone was too busy.

Victoria set up her camera in front of the van, where she had a clear shot of the picturesque storm. Roan set up his a few feet away, turned it on, and left it. He then concentrated on still shots with his Nikon and an incredibly long lens. A lone Guernsey cow watched curiously from the other side of a fence.

Just when the chasers were beginning to grumble that it might not happen after all, a funnel dropped out of the wall cloud. Thin and hesitant at first, the spindly twister reached for the ground, touched down, and kicked up a small puff of debris.

Even though Victoria had seen dozens of tornadoes, her heart beat wildly with each, this one included. She estimated it was a couple of miles away and moving almost due north, while the chasers had gathered well to the east. Their position couldn't have been better.

The narrow, cone-shaped funnel seemed to have an ethereal glow all its own, and it pulsated from top to bottom. An eerie hush fell over the participants as the tornado moved along, kicking up fence posts like toothpicks and uprooting the few scraggly trees in its path.

All at once the twister seemed to stop moving. Bothered by this, Victoria leaned into the van's open window to listen to the radio. The spotters reported that the storm was no longer moving due north, but had taken an abrupt turn eastward—which meant it was heading straight for them.

Other chasers had apparently learned the same thing, for a concerned murmur moved among them. Almost as one the group seemed to decide it was time to beat a hasty retreat, and Victoria agreed. While the twister was still a safe distance away, she wasn't going to take any chances. She grabbed her camera and quickly mounted it back on the dash.

Roan was now behind his videocamera, describing aloud what was going on for the benefit of the video soundtrack.

"Roan, we have to go now," Victoria announced. Already, car engines were starting as the fastest of the group prepared to make an escape.

Roan turned to look at her, clearly baffled. "Go? Why?"

"Because we're in the path of the storm."

"I thought it was moving north."

"That's changed. Come on, grab your camera and let's go."

Roan looked around at the exodus in progress. Then he focused on one car in particular, a beat-up Volkswagen Rabbit that didn't seem to be going anywhere. "Those guys are staying," he said, pointing.

"John Higgenbotham and Dave Devors," Victoria said, her voice thick with disapproval. "Meteorology students from Texas Tech. They have no idea what they're doing. Take a look at the hail dents in their car. That should tell you something."

"Mmm," Roan said noncommittally as he returned his attention to his camera and the spectacle taking place before them. "Just a few more minutes. We're not in any imminent danger."

"If we aren't now, we will be soon. C'mon, Roan, I don't like cutting it this close."

"Relax, we have plenty of time," he said distractedly.

There were now only a few cars remaining. Even the TV van had hightailed it to a safer vantage point. The wind was kicking into high gear, blowing dust and dried grass. A chill came over Victoria as she remembered another time when she'd stood in the face of such a wind.

"Roan, that's enough already." She was getting mad now that he wasn't listening to her. "We have to go, or we're going to get ourselves killed."

"Just another minute."

Victoria watched as the two students packed it in, whooping and hollering in high spirits. That did it. Perhaps Roan didn't understand the danger, but she did.

"Roan!" She stepped in front of his camera and put her hand over the lens. "You get your butt into that van this second, or I'm leaving without you!" She had to shout to be heard over the roaring wind, but she would have shouted anyway. She couldn't remember ever feeling so angry at anyone.

Without another word he grabbed the camera, tripod and all, and jumped into the van, barely ahead of the first barrage of rain.

Victoria was already behind the steering wheel. She fumbled with the key, finally managing to insert it into the ignition. But in her anxiety she cranked it too hard, gave it too much gas.

"Easy, Vic, you're gonna flood the engine."

"Just shut up," she snapped. "I know how to drive." But she was so flustered, she repeated her mistake. The engine caught, gave a mighty roar, then died. "Dammit!" She was shaking now, but she forced herself to take her foot off the gas and slowly, gently, turn the key. The engine coughed, caught again, died.

After three more attempts, the van finally started. But it was too late. Except for the cow, who was now pacing back and forth behind the fence, they were the only ones left on the deserted stretch of road. Everyone else had fled south, but the tornado was poised to move across the road, cutting off that particular escape route. No place to go but north, and Victoria remembered something about a dirt road in that direction.

She backed onto the pavement, threw the van in forward gear, and floored it. Roan put on his seat belt without a reminder, and Victoria realized she'd forgotten hers. To hell with it. If the tornado squashed the van flat, a seat belt wouldn't do her much good anyway.

The paved road soon deteriorated to gravel, then dirt. Then it disappeared altogether, petering out at the edge of a creek.

Roan looked out the back window. "Oh, *hell.* It's heading right for us." Rather than sounding worried, he sounded excited.

"No kidding!"

"Well, what do we do?"

She switched off the engine. "Nothing. The van is the only cover we have, so we huddle here and pray the twister doesn't kill us." Small hail was now pelting the van.

"Maybe it would be safer if we got in back, away from the windows," Roan suggested, for the first time sounding slightly apprehensive.

He ought to be downright terrified, Victoria thought. The wind roared around the van, shaking it violently, and the rain and hail made it sound as though they were sitting under a waterfall. They would be lucky if all they suffered was broken windows. He did have a point, though, about moving into the back of the van.

Roan reclined his seat and crawled over it with no more trouble than a cat would have had, then helped Victoria perform the same maneuver. Unfortunately she was less graceful, very nearly sliding into his lap. He grabbed her around the waist and steadied her until she found her footing. As angry as she was with him, she found the warmth of his touch reassuring in the face of danger, and she wished he didn't have to let her go.

The hail was larger now, at least quarter-sized. It looked like popcorn bouncing around, but it sounded more like a machine gun as it hit the van with sharp staccato cracks. The combined rain and hail had become so thick that Victoria could no longer see the tornado when she looked out the back window, but that didn't mean it wasn't there.

A loud boom of thunder rattled the van, and Victoria couldn't contain her fear any longer. She began to shiver and couldn't stop, no matter how tightly she wrapped her arms around herself, and her breathing came in quick, irregular gasps. She felt like that twelve-year-old girl again, terrified and helpless.

Roan's arm stole around her shoulders. "Easy, Vic, we're gonna make it through this. I'm sure it sounds worse than it is."

Spoken like a true ignoramus, she wanted to say. He truly had no idea how much danger they were in. But oddly, perversely, she liked the feel of his arms around her. She wanted to duck her head against his broad shoulder, bury her face against his soft cotton T-shirt, lose her terror by losing herself in his masculine scent.

And that's exactly what she did. When the hail grew to golf-ball size, thunking against the roof of the van in a deafening barrage and cracking the windshield, she no longer cared whether she appeared foolish. She just wanted to believe in the myth that his strong arms could protect her. He tightened his hold on her and stroked her hair, murmuring soothing inanities.

"I had no idea you would be so frightened," he said when she'd stopped trembling. "Why do you chase storms if they scare you so much?"

"It's not for the thrill."

"Then why?" he persisted.

She hesitated. It felt nice in the shelter of his arms, and telling him what he wanted to know would spoil it. Then she remembered that he was the one who'd gotten them into this mess. She wouldn't have needed his comfort if he hadn't delayed until their escape route had been cut off. Whether she wanted to tell him the whole dang story or not, she needed to. She had to make him understand, in a personal way, how close to harm they were. So she plunged ahead, her voice low in spite of the barrage of noise.

"One spring afternoon, when I was twelve years old, we had a tornado. It was totally unexpected—we knew nothing about it until the sirens went off. I had to run out in the storm to warn my father. He was on his tractor, plowing, and he was almost deaf, so he wouldn't have heard the warning.

"I was only a few hundred feet away, trying to get to him in time." She swallowed. "Then something hit me in the head—a piece of flying debris, maybe a tree branch. I was never sure. It knocked me out for a few seconds. And when I came to, the tractor was gone. My father was gone."

Roan said nothing. The only clue she had that he'd even heard her was the slight acceleration in his breathing, the almost undetectable increase of tension in his body.

She hesitated, not sure how much she wanted to tell him. But talking took her mind off the current situation, so she continued, trying not to worry so much about whether she was revealing too much about herself.

"As soon as the shock wore off, I became really angry that the Weather Service hadn't warned us sooner. And then I started wondering why the twister took my father and left me alone. All of that turned into a sort of obsession with tornadoes. I wanted to learn everything I could about them, especially the prediction part, so that maybe my efforts could save a life someday. But no matter how many storms I go through—and I've been through a bunch—I always remember that day, the helplessness, the fear. . . ."

He rubbed her shoulder. "I'm sorry."

She shook off his attempt at comfort. "I'm not looking for pity. You wanted to understand, so I told you."

"What I understand is that you're very brave."

"Oh, give me a break."

"No, really. I might do a lot of daring things, but that's because I'm not afraid. You, on the other hand, do daring things despite your fear. That makes what you do a hundred times braver than what I do."

"I don't care whether anyone thinks I'm brave or not." She thought a moment, then added, "That's where you and I differ. Markedly."

"You think I do what I do because I want people to think I'm brave?" he asked incredulously.

"Isn't that a big part of it?"

He merely shook his head, but he offered no further argument.

The storm had passed. The rain was now a gentle patter on the roof. The wind had died down, the thunder and lightning were reduced to distant rumbles. With the return of safety came the return of her sanity. She lifted her head from Roan's shoulder and made a show of pulling away from him. Impulsively she picked up the road atlas and thumped him with it.

He stared at her, his mouth hanging open. "What was that for?"

"You almost got us killed, that's what!"

"Are you saying the tornado was my fault?"

"I'm saying that if you'd gotten in the van when I first told you to," she said in a calmer tone of voice, "we would have gone south and been out of the way in plenty of time."

He flashed his most beguiling smile. "Oh, now, there was really no harm done—"

"Don't you use that patronizing tone with me. You promised Amos, and you promised me that you would cooperate with me completely. You didn't. And if you think there was no harm done—" She turned and opened the sliding side door of the van and hopped to the ground. "The roof has hail dents all over it, and the windshield is cracked. I promised Amos I wouldn't let anything happen to the Chasemobile."

Roan climbed out of the van to survey the damage. "It's supposed to have a few hail dents. As I recall, his old truck was peppered with them."

"This is different."

"How so?"

"It could have been prevented."

"Do you want an apology? Is that what you're angling for?"

They stood in the light rain, staring at each other like a couple of cats ready to fight. Victoria's hands were on her hips, Roan's arms were folded.

"An apology would be nice," she said quietly.

"All right, I'm sorry. I thought you were being overcautious."

As apologies went, it wasn't the most gracious Victoria had ever heard. But she had a feeling those few terse words were all she was going to get.

"Fine," she said, walking around to the driver's door. "Let's just get out of here."

"Where are we going?" he asked.

"Lubbock—at the first opportunity. Your storm-chasing days are over."

Victoria slowed the van down as they passed the part of the road where the tornado had come through. Roan had never seen tornado damage up close, and he stared out the windows wide-eyed as he surveyed the uprooted trees, the ripped-up fence . . . and the dead cow, lying in a ditch.

"What . . ." Roan began to say, but his throat was so dry, he had to clear it and begin again. "What happened to the cow?"

Victoria shrugged. "Probably hit by debris, poor thing."

Roan felt a chill move through him. If he had procrastinated another few minutes, even another few seconds, their fate could have been similar to the cow's.

"Victoria, I'm . . . I really am sorry. I had no idea the danger we were in. Besides that, I showed total disrespect for your knowledge, your—"

"Groveling will get you nowhere, Roan. I'm taking you back to Lubbock."

He couldn't blame her, not at all. "You don't have to take me all the way to Lubbock. Just let me off anywhere and I'll get back on my own. That way, you won't have to interrupt your chase trip."

"I can't chase alone anyway," she said resignedly.

"Maybe in a few days Amos will be feeling better and we can sneak in another trip before my vacation is over. That is if there's anything to chase. Anyway, I don't think Amos would appreciate it if I dumped off his favorite nephew in the middle of the road."

And that was probably all that was preventing her from doing just that, Roan mused. He'd really blown it, and all because he'd been so caught up in the beauty and power of the storm that he couldn't tear himself away.

When had he become so self-centered? It was bad enough he had almost convinced Victoria to bungee jump. But his behavior with the storm had been far worse. He had shown total disregard for his own life and Victoria's. He ought to be horse-whipped.

They listened in silence to the various radios as excited voices dissected the tornado, which had stayed on the ground at least twelve minutes and had caused considerable crop damage, although no one had been injured—not counting the cow. There was some desultory conversation about another promising storm a few miles west, but if Victoria heard it, she chose to ignore it.

"Hungry?" she asked, the word clipped.

"Sure," he replied, though for once he really didn't have much appetite.

"I'll drive north a ways and find some restaurant where there's no chance of running into other chasers. I'm not much in the mood for chitchat."

"Sure, whatever."

She didn't utter another word during the next twenty minutes. Roan knew she was mad, but he also suspected she might be a little embarrassed about confiding in him during a weak moment.

"Does anyone else know you're afraid of storms?" he asked suddenly, breaking the silence.

"Amos has seen me lose it a time or two, but he's never asked any questions."

"And I should follow his example, right?"

"Please."

They had entered some little town whose name never registered in Roan's mind, and Victoria pulled the van into the parking lot of a motel with a restaurant next door.

"At least we finally get to eat steak," she muttered as they got out. Roan sensed a slight softening, a blur around the sharp edges of her anger. He decided not to risk further antagonizing her by teasing or cajoling. She would eventually come out of her temper if he gave her enough room. He didn't think she was the type to hold a grudge for long.

"Yeah, I'm looking forward to a nice porterhouse, or maybe a T-bone," he said cheerfully, though he didn't mean it. Food was the furthest thing from his mind.

A waitress seated them in a booth at the back of the restaurant. Without opening the menu, Victoria ordered the smallest available steak, which turned out to be a petite cut fillet, and a loaded baked potato. Roan said he would have the same. But when their food arrived a few minutes later, he found he couldn't stomach even one bite of the tender, succulent beef. He didn't feel he deserved a reward of any kind.

EIGHT

By the time she'd eaten a good portion of steak and almost all of her baked potato, Victoria was feeling marginally better. She'd been much too emotional earlier, she decided. Consequently she'd blown the afternoon's incident all out of proportion. Roan had behaved like an ass, but he'd realized his mistake and had apologized for it. She was convinced of his sincerity, and it would serve no purpose to spitefully punish him by returning to Lubbock.

Unless he wanted to go back. Maybe now that he'd gotten some video footage, he was fed up with the whole storm-chasing thing. That thought filled Victoria with unexpected melancholy.

"Do you want to split a piece of apple pie?" she asked, determined to put the unpleasantness behind her and start fresh with Roan.

He met her gaze briefly, then looked away. "No, thanks."

"Not even à la mode?"

"No. I'm full. But you go ahead."

Full? She studied his plate. He'd cut his steak up into tiny pieces and pushed it around on his plate, but he hadn't eaten much of anything. "Are you feeling all right?" she couldn't help asking.

He managed a faint smile. "I'm fine, Victoria. Just not hungry."

Victoria. Not "Vicky" or "Vic." And he hadn't stumbled or hesitated over all four syllables either. Perversely, she missed the pet name. She'd gotten used to it. Had she finally alienated him for good? Had he given up teasing her? Where were his playful smiles, his brash, outrageous behavior?

When she'd forced him to look at the tornado damage and acknowledge the danger they'd been in, she'd intended only to shake him up a little, not send him into a major depression. But there was definitely something wrong, something beyond fatigue and a loss of appetite. She'd only sensed a sadness in him before, but now she could see it in every line of his face, every gesture he made.

"Do you want to talk about it?" she asked impulsively.

He looked up sharply, like he'd been caught doing something he shouldn't, then flashed what looked to Victoria like a forced smile. "What's there to talk about? I screwed up. I'll suffer the consequences. It's nothing new to me."

"Do you screw up a lot?" she asked, finding that hard to believe. Although at times he could be a pain in the butt, he never struck her as anything but utterly competent.

"Doesn't everyone? And the world's not a very forgiving place."

She was shocked. No, she was beyond that. This was a side of Roan Cullen she'd never seen, had never suspected existed beneath the happy-go-lucky surface. Rather than being put off by his moroseness, she was intrigued . . . and maybe a little guilty for having heaped so much hostility on him when he was more vulnerable than she'd thought. She wanted to know what was at the core of his sadness.

Not that she had any right to know. Just because she'd spilled her guts to him—what in the world had made her do that?—didn't mean he had to follow suit. Whatever his deep secrets were, they were none of her business.

Still, the fact that she had confided in him had created a certain degree of intimacy between them. She at least had a right to be concerned about him, if not privy to his thoughts.

When the waitress returned to clear the table, Victoria ordered pie, hoping Roan would steal a few bites from her plate as he'd done during their first dinner together. But he showed no interest in the dessert.

"I wonder what's in store for tomorrow," she ventured to ask. "Three tornadoes in three days. That's pretty unusual. At this rate—and with a little luck—it could be a very successful chase trip."

"I thought a straight shot to Lubbock was the only thing on our agenda." Roan eyed her warily.

"Well, yeah, but if there's anything really promising on the way there, I want to know about it. No sense foregoing a good storm if it's close at hand."

Roan looked the tiniest bit hopeful. "I'll take care of the check if you want to get a head start doing your computer thing."

"Thanks, I think I will." She started to reach into her purse for some money, but he shook his head.

"It's my turn."

She wasn't sure that it was, but it struck her that allowing him to pay might give him a small injection of machismo, and perhaps restore a little of his old spirit.

By the time Roan had joined her in the van a few minutes later, she'd seen enough. The storms were all played out for the time being. She'd be willing to bet her last ten bucks that tomorrow there wouldn't be a decent storm anywhere in Tornado Alley.

So much for her only excuse for postponing the trip back to Lubbock. This would be the perfect time to get rid of Roan, when there was virtually no chance she would miss something.

"Anything interesting?" Roan asked.

"Not sure yet," she hedged. She shut down the computer and stacked her scribbled-up maps in a basket beside the printer. "Let's find a motel and crash. I'm beat. Maybe things will look more promising in the morning." And she wasn't just talking about the weather.

Roan had to rub his bleary eyes as he waited for the motel clerk to give him a receipt. A night of tossing and turning hadn't done his disposition any good. He'd relived yesterday's events over and over, wondering if he'd really been as reckless as he remembered. And when he'd managed to fall asleep, he'd suffered vague, unsettling nightmares interspersed with erotic dreams about wrapping his naked body in long, auburn hair.

The thirty seconds of hot water in the shower, followed by ice cold spray, had put a cap on his morning outlook. He had Victoria to thank for that. He'd spotted a perfectly charming bed and breakfast in town, but she had to have her cable TV. And this fleabag motel was the only local lodging that fit the bill.

Immediately he felt guilty for his spite. Victoria had certain criteria she had to follow, and it wasn't fair of him to begrudge her the Weather Channel. He supposed he was grouchy because she was sending him home in disgrace. He didn't even want to think about how he would explain things to Amos.

He couldn't blame Victoria. Hell, he hadn't even tried to talk her out of the decision, because he knew she was perfectly justified in giving him the boot.

He was surprised at how disappointed he felt. After all, he'd gotten what he came for. He'd experienced a tornado and he'd captured what he hoped were some damn good photos. It was time to move on to something else.

But he hadn't realized how much he'd been looking forward to spending more time with Victoria. Even if he had promised he wouldn't lay a hand on her, he still enjoyed her company.

When she met him at the van a few minutes later, she was subdued, but not all tight and angry like she'd been the night before. She appeared rested at least.

"Have you checked the data this morning?" he asked.

She nodded glumly as she stowed her gear in the back of the van. "Looks awful. We don't have a prayer of finding any action."

"Oh." Hell. He'd been hoping for some little storm somewhere to distract Victoria from her goal of dumping him off in Lubbock. He'd thought that maybe, if he became a model of cooperation, she would relent. So much for that idea.

"Do you want to go back to Lubbock?" she asked suddenly, reading his mind again. She amazed him with her ability to tap into his thoughts, and she didn't even know she was doing it.

He felt the urge to lie and save his pride. He almost said, Sure, whatever you think, as if it didn't make that much difference to him. But looking at her, taking in those big hazel eyes, the petal-soft skin of her cheek, and her long, denim-clad legs, he couldn't say he wanted to leave her. He couldn't just toss off some careless rejoinder.

"No," he said slowly, deliberately, "I don't want to go back to Lubbock."

"I thought maybe you'd be tired of storm chasing by now. It's pretty boring sometimes."

"And I thought you were tired of me," he countered, managing a grin.

"Exasperated, maybe, but never tired of you. You aren't a boring person, Roan Cullen."

Was this possible? Was she actually going to give him a reprieve? "In that case, I definitely don't want to go back to Lubbock."

"Okay. But I warn you, you might not like the alternative. I talked to Amos this morning. He seems to think, and I agree, that if anything develops, it will be north—Kansas, Nebraska, maybe Missouri. Have you ever been to Nebraska?"

"No."

"Well, Nebraska is my old stomping grounds. My mother still lives on the farm where I grew up. I thought we could pay her a visit, keep an eye on the weather from there, and be ready to take off if something does develop. But meanwhile we'll be comfortable, and we'll save money on motels. Those are your choices—Lubbock, or my mother's." She slammed the van's back door, then crossed her arms and gave Roan a challenging stare.

The choice was easy. Anything would have been preferable to returning to Lubbock, but a visit to a Nebraska farm sounded surprisingly appealing.

"You're sure your mother won't mind an uninvited guest?" he asked.

"Not at all. There's plenty of room, and she's a great cook. She's always complaining that she never gets to cook for anyone but herself, and that's no fun."

"In that case, sure, let's go for the farm."

Victoria nodded, but she looked a bit worried. Maybe she was nervous about his meeting her mother, although she shouldn't be. It wasn't as if she were bringing home a new boyfriend. At any rate, he wouldn't give her anything to worry about.

Their destination, a town called Eads, was only four hours away. Roan enjoyed the countryside, although Nebraska, when they got there, didn't look much different from Kansas—flat farmland, old barns and white frame houses, windmills, and little towns that were all blending together in his mind.

Eads looked just like the others, a wide place on the highway lined with aging storefronts, with more modern buildings, a big discount store, and fast-food restaurants on the outskirts. When they hit Main Street, Victoria turned the van off the highway. They passed a quaint little town square, a generic-looking high school, a well-tended cemetery.

Victoria offered brief comments about each point of interest. Roan nodded as her honey-smooth voice washed over him, less concerned with the town's history than he was about the fact that Victoria was no longer mad at him. He wished, for the umpteenth time in as many minutes, that he hadn't promised not to touch her. But he'd already broken his word once to her, when he'd ignored her attempts to get them out of the way of the tornado. He wouldn't break another promise no matter how badly he wanted to.

At last they ended up on a winding tree-lined country road that dead-ended in front of a small, neat white frame house with kelly-green shutters. A large, mongrel-like dog rushed out to meet the van, barking wildly and wagging his whole rear end.

"This is the place," Victoria said as she cut the motor. "I hope that famous appetite of yours is in full swing, because Mother will stuff you to the gills."

"Great. I'm ready for lunch."

A petite woman with frizzy blond hair rushed out on the front porch to meet them, and Roan realized with a start that she was Victoria's mother. He had pictured someone tall and dignified, an older version of Victoria with silver-streaked hair pulled back in a bun, maybe wearing an apron.

Nelva Driscoll was a head shorter than her daughter. And she was wearing a tennis dress. She wrapped Victoria in a fluttery hug. "Oh, honey, it's good to see you. I just this minute got back from my tennis game and got your message." She turned her blue-eyed gaze on Roan. "And this must be Professor Amos's nephew. I'm sorry, Victoria neglected to mention your name."

"Roan Cullen," he said, extending his hand. "It's nice to meet you, Mrs. Driscoll."

She shook it vigorously, and he got the impression that if he'd been at all encouraging, she would have hugged him. "Now, let's not be so formal. You call me Nelva. Oh, it's so good to have both of you here. Victoria, why don't you get Roan settled in the guest cottage while I take a shower? Then we'll see about dinner. You haven't had dinner, have you?"

"No, Mother," Victoria said with a fond smile. "I know better than to eat before I get here." She turned to Roan and added, "She means lunch. In this part of the country, lunch is dinner and dinner is supper."

After a few more directives about where to find sheets and towels, Nelva left for her shower. Victoria and Roan got their bags from the van. She left hers on the front porch, then led him along a stone-paved path to a little cabin sheltered in a grove of trees.

"You have a guest house," Roan said. "I'm impressed."

"Don't be impressed until you see the inside. It actually used to be a caretaker's cottage. My grandparents lived here for a while when I was little."

"Grandparents." He leaned against the porch railing. "I always wanted grandparents, but they all died before I was born. Are yours still living?"

"Just one grandpa. He's ninety-three and lives in a nursing home, but he's still pretty with it up here." She tapped her temple with one forefinger.

"Wow. Ninety-three. I don't think anyone in my family has lived that long. Uncle Amos holds the record."

"If they're all like you, I'm not surprised," she quipped, then immediately slapped her hand over her mouth. "I'm sorry. That was tacky."

"But true. We Cullens do tend to live fast and hard. It's a family joke that no Cullen is allowed to die of natural causes." He couldn't help the bitter edge that crept into his voice.

She reached above the door frame and retrieved a key. But she paused in the act of unlocking the door. "Your sister who died—was that an accident?"

Kim. Memories of that awful day had been nibbling at his subconscious since the day before, but rather than dwelling on them, as he usually did, he'd managed to push them aside. Now Victoria's innocent question hit him in the chest with the force of a cement truck going full throttle.

An accident? No, it was a deliberate act of negligence. Reckless disregard for safety. "She died scuba diving," he said gruffly.

Victoria looked up at him, her expression stricken. "God, that's awful. I'm so sorry. I shouldn't have brought it up." She twisted the key and pushed open the door. "Ugh, it's musty in here. Let's open the windows and air it out." Roan watched her unlock and hurl open every window in the place until she got to one in the bedroom that was stuck. She strained and heaved, breathing heavily.

He came up behind her. "Let me try."

"No! I can get it."

He grasped her by the shoulders and pulled her away, knowing her distress wasn't about the window. "Vic, it's okay. You haven't said anything wrong."

She folded her arms around herself and hung her head. "Yes, I did. I hate it when people ask me about my father, wanting to know the details of why he died so young. I should know better than to ask morbidly curious questions."

"It's okay," he said again. "I'm the one who brought up the subject of death in the family. It was a perfectly natural question, not morbidly curious. But it isn't something I can talk about."

"I understand. Consider the subject dropped." They both went for the window, bumping shoulders. Victoria danced out of the way, as if she'd been branded with a hot poker.

Roan silently shook his head, understanding just how she felt. Being so close and not being able to touch was eating at him. He'd been around desirable women who were off-limits before, and his solution had always been to get the heck away from them. But with Victoria, he found he was willing to endure the torture of unfulfilled lust just to be near her.

That said something about her appeal. Or maybe it simply said something about his need for female companionship. How long had it been since he'd allowed himself to enjoy a woman's company on any level? So long, he'd forgotten.

Victoria found a stack of white sheets in the hall cupboard and set about making the bed. Roan tried to help, but every time he looked at her on the opposite side of the mattress, he felt an overwhelming urge to reach across and drag her down to those crisp white sheets. Eventually he settled for putting cases on the pillows, leaving the sheets and blankets to her.

By the time they returned to the main house, Nelva had changed into jeans and a Texas Tech T-shirt and was attending to several simmering pots on the stove. "I hope you don't mind leftovers," she said. "It's just some sliced roast beef and gravy over rice."

"It smells wonderful," Roan said sincerely. Real home cooking. How long had it been since he'd indulged in that, other than when he'd eaten Victoria's chicken soup?

Two of his favorite things, women and good cooking, and he'd been denying himself. Was it accidental? Or had he done it on purpose? What other of life's pleasures had he deliberately avoided in the past three years?

"Is there something we can do to help?" Victoria asked.

"You can set the table," Nelva said. "And put ice in the glasses for tea."

"I can do the ice part," Roan said.

Victoria gave him a look that said she was surprised at his sudden streak of domesticity. Well, he could be as civilized as the next guy when he wanted to be. And for some odd reason, at the moment he really wanted to be.

Lunch was delicious, and Nelva was a delight, although Roan couldn't recall ever seeing a mother and daughter such polar opposites in looks as well as personality. Nelva was as bubbly as Victoria was reserved. She was a toucher too, constantly reaching across the table to touch Victoria's arm. She even did that a couple of times with him.

Nelva inquired after Amos's health and then asked all about the chase trip so far. When Victoria mumbled something like "Yeah, we saw one little twister, no big deal," Nelva turned to Roan.

"It might not be a big deal to Miss Meteorologist over here," she said in a loud stage whisper, nodding toward her daughter, "but I'll bet you were thrilled. Was this the first time you ever saw a tornado?"

"Yes, it was. And it was exciting." Maybe a little too. "I'll be interested to see the video footage. In fact . . . do you have a VCR?"

"Sure I do. That's a great idea. Victoria never lets me watch her videotapes."

Victoria was shaking her head at Roan, and suddenly he realized why. Good Lord, how insensitive could he be? This woman's husband had been killed by a tornado, and he was asking her to *watch* one?

"Um, maybe later," he said.

"I don't think that's a good idea," Victoria said at the same time. They both stopped and looked at each other self-consciously.

"What's wrong with you two?" Nelva asked. Then she winked and said, "Don't tell me. You've got some X-rated footage mixed up with the storm videos, and you're afraid it'll pop up on the TV screen—"

"Mother! That's not even—I mean, I never—"

"Oh, stop blustering." Nelva nudged Victoria on the arm. She looked at Roan. "Honestly, the girl did not inherit her sense of humor from me." But she grew more serious as she turned back to her daughter. "Do you think I don't know why you've never shown me your tornado pictures? Victoria honey, your father's been dead for eighteen years. Sure he was killed by a tornado. But if I got misty-eyed over every storm that passes over, I'd be the gloomiest lady in town. Trust me, watching a movie of a tornado isn't going to send me into a weeping frenzy. One tornado was responsible for your father's death, and I can't hold it against all of them. You don't, do you?"

"Well, no," Victoria agreed. "But sometimes, in certain situations, I still think of him." Her gaze caught and held with Roan's for a fraction of a second, and he knew she was remembering when they'd been caught in the hailstorm and she'd felt so helpless.

"Come on," Nelva urged, "go get your tapes. I want to see them."

Victoria finally consented, and Roan went out to the van to get both tapes. He sat on the couch between Victoria and her mother as they watched. Victoria would have stopped the tape before the part where they got into their argument, but Roan wouldn't let her. He wanted to burn the scene into his brain—just in case he was ever tempted to forget—so he would never act like such a jerk again.

Only when Victoria stepped in front of the camera, cursing up a blue streak, did Roan stop the tape.

"Goodness, Victoria, I didn't know you could cuss like that," Nelva said.

Victoria turned six shades of pink. "I didn't either. I don't even remember saying all those things."

"Believe me, it was appropriate to the situation," Roan said, feeling uncomfortable at reliving the scene. But he'd already apologized at least twice, and he wasn't going to again.

Nelva laughed. "You know, Roan, I think you're a good influence on Victoria. I always said she needed to loosen up a little."

"Mother, please . . ."

Ordinarily Roan would have laughed at Victoria's discomfiture. But not when he knew he was anything but a good influence on her. The videotape had just reminded him of that.

Except for a few rough spots, Victoria thought the day went smoothly. Roan was polite, respectful, and thoroughly civilized—everything she'd thought he wasn't capable of. In short, he wasn't being himself, and it bothered the heck out of her. She couldn't escape the feeling that she was responsible for his change of behavior.

She found herself wishing her mother could see the Roan she knew. The two of them had the same kind of offbeat sense of humor, and she knew her mother would have appreciated his irreverence—more than Victoria herself had in the beginning.

Roan did loosen up enough to regale her mother with some of his more daring escapades. Since Victoria wasn't supposed to bolster Roan's death-defying behavior, she had never encouraged him to talk about his adventures. But Nelva had no such qualms, and she egged Roan on, laughing at the more amusing tight spots he'd gotten himself into, showing appropriate horror over his brushes with death.

For his part, Roan recounted his experiences matter-of-factly, with none of the swagger she'd expected from him.

Victoria couldn't help being fascinated by his stories, but they also scared the bejeezus out of her. How could someone take the gift of life so lightly? Either he'd never outgrown that adolescent belief in immortality, or he just didn't care. She was beginning to believe it was the latter.

After an early supper, Nelva suggested they play crazy eights. Victoria was all for it. She hadn't played that game in years—since high school—and she could remember laughing with her friends over a messy table full of cards. Laughter was such a healing thing.

But Roan declined. He thanked Victoria's mother for the fine dinner, made some excuse about wanting to do a little reading, and left for the guest cottage.

Victoria watched him go, puzzled. What was bothering him? Her mother stared after him, a speculative gleam in her eye. "Where has your professor been hiding this nephew all these years?"

"Now, Mother, don't start. Nothing is going on between Roan and me, and nothing will."

"Whyever not? He's gorgeous."

"There's more to life than good looks."

"Okay, what's wrong with him?" Nelva challenged.

"You have to ask, after listening to those stories of his? He obviously doesn't sit still long enough to have a relationship. And even if he did—would you want to fall in love with someone who's probably going to kill himself with those idiotic stunts he pulls?"

"Victoria honey . . ." Nelva led her daughter to the couch, and they both sat down. "I married a nice, safe Nebraska farmer, and look what happened to him. You can't predict these things, and you can't live in fear of them. If I had somehow known that your father would be taken from me in his prime, I still would have married him. I treasure the years we did have together."

Victoria smiled, as she always did when she thought about the strong love between her parents. And that gave her the perfect argument. "Roan and I aren't in love the way you and Daddy were. I'm not even sure we like each other all that much."

"Since you've known each other for only four days, I'm sure you're not in love," Nelva agreed. "But you could at least give it a chance. You always analyze any halfway decent guy to death, until you come up with a reason why you shouldn't even give it a try. You've been like that since puberty."

Victoria sighed. They'd covered this territory before. "Trust me on this one, Mother. Roan and I are as different as night and day. We disagree constantly, we have nothing in common—"

"Sounds like your father and me," Nelva said. "You inherited all your caution and common sense from him, you know. I was the crazy one. People thought our marriage would never work."

"Mother . . ."

"Okay, okay. Do you still want to play cards?"

"How 'bout we just watch an old movie?"

Nelva dug out a 1930s screwball comedy with Katharine Hepburn and Cary Grant, which gave Victoria a couple of hours of mindless enjoyment. But after her mother went to bed, Victoria's thoughts turned to Roan again, as they had far too often these past few days. She wondered what he was doing. Was he really reading, or had he simply wanted some time away from her?

After slipping into a knee-length T-shirt she'd found in a drawer in her old bedroom, Victoria sat cross-legged on her bed and pulled up the latest weather data on her laptop computer. But there was nothing very interesting going on, and more than once she found her gaze straying out the window, where she had a perfect view of the guest cottage. When the lights went off, she pictured Roan lying in the bed they'd made up, the snowy sheets contrasting against his tanned skin. The image sent a shock of awareness coursing through her. When had she become so . . . so lustful?

She closed the computer and looked out the window again. This time she saw a faint orange pin of light she knew was the end of a cigarette. He was sitting on the porch, smoking. Alone. In the dark.

Prudent or not, cautious or not, it wasn't in Victoria's makeup to ignore a creature in pain. And she knew, as surely as she knew her shoe size, that Roan was hurting. She'd thought at first he was just smarting from the tongue-lashing she'd given him, but he wouldn't still be brooding about that.

Unable to talk herself out of it, she found an old velour robe and tied it tightly about herself, more in deference to the evening chill than modesty. She couldn't seem to locate any shoes, so she slipped out the kitchen door with nothing but socks to protect her feet from the damp ground and picked her way through the dark toward the cottage.

She couldn't very well hide her approach. Roan had to have seen her coming from a hundred feet away, but he didn't move.

"What are you doing here?" he asked flatly when she got close enough.

"Visiting. Move over."

He obliged by scooting over to give her room to sit on the top porch step beside him. As she sat down, she saw the glowing arc of his cigarette as he tossed it over the railing. It was on the tip of her tongue to remind him about fires, but she stopped herself. The ground was wet, and the ember was probably extinguished the moment it fell.

Besides, she was much more concerned about the fact that Roan wasn't wearing a shirt. "Aren't you cold?" she asked. The temperature had already dropped into the fifties.

"A little."

"Why don't you get a shirt?"

"Because I like to be cold, okay?"

His surliness silenced her, but only for a moment. "You know, you haven't been yourself since . . . well, since we argued."

"Has my behavior given you anything to complain about?"

"No, I didn't come here to complain."

"Then why are you here?"

"Because I'm concerned. And I feel like I've done something to upset you—"

"Other than blowing your stack at me?"

"You had that coming, and I don't think that's the problem anyway. I feel like I've done something else, but I don't know what it could be."

"What makes you so sure I'm 'upset,' as you put it?"

"I can tell. Give me some credit."

"Yeah, well, whatever's wrong, don't flatter yourself. It's got nothing to do with you."

Victoria refused to let his words hurt her. She was sure he was trying to drive her away, and she wouldn't be driven. "What is wrong, then? I'll understand if you don't want to talk about it—"

"I don't want to talk about it."

A supercharged silence stretched between them, growing more taut by the second. Victoria had to resist a powerful urge to touch Roan, to offer comfort even if she didn't understand why he was hurting. But she knew from recent experience how quickly comfort could turn into passion.

She tried to think of something to say, something that would ease them out of the awkward silence. But Roan beat her to it.

"Do you really want to know what's on my mind?" he asked bitterly. "Do you honestly want to find out what kind of selfish bastard I am?"

The harshness in his voice scared her. Maybe she didn't want to know. But regardless of whether she did, she sensed that Roan needed to tell her. "Yes. I want to know what's troubling you."

He sighed heavily. "We were talking earlier about my sister. My baby sister, twenty-two years old. She died scuba diving, but it wasn't an accident.

"I killed her."

NINE

Roan knew he'd shocked her. As dark as it was, he could see that her eyes were huge and full of questions.

"I don't believe it," she finally said.

"It's true."

"Explain it to me."

He heaved another great sigh. The incident was as familiar to him as his own face in the mirror. He could recite the facts in his sleep. Not that he would enjoy telling the story, but if that's what it took to make her go away and leave him in peace . . .

"I was in Australia, working on some photos of the Great Barrier Reef for *Nature* magazine, and Kim decided to come visit me. We were never very close, what with the age difference and all, and I thought this would be a great chance for us to get to know each other, adult to adult."

Roan stared out into nothingness as he spoke, turning over the painful images in his mind the way a kid overturns rocks to see what squirmy things lurk underneath.

"I'd been doing some underwater photography, and I wanted to show her the incredible things I'd seen. She was a good swimmer, but she was afraid to swim in the ocean.

"I badgered her for a couple of days, promised her over and over that nothing would happen to her as long as she was with me. Finally I talked her into it. I think in the end she gave in because she didn't want me to think she was a wimp.

"Anyway, I took her to a calm cove first, and when that went okay we went into deeper waters. Lots deeper. It was way too challenging for a first-time diver, but she was doing so well, I didn't give it a second thought. I really believed that nothing could touch her as long as big brother was there to protect her."

He paused to chance a look at Victoria. She was all rapt attention, leaning closer to catch his hushed words. He could smell a soft, undefinable scent that was hers alone.

"We were about seventy feet down when Kim somehow breathed in a mouthful of water. She signaled me that she was in trouble, and her first instinct was to shoot for the surface, but I stopped her because I didn't want her to get the bends. So we made a slow, controlled ascent, and she was gripping my hand so hard . . .

"About halfway to the surface, I felt her grip loosen. And when we finally made it, her face was blue and she was unconscious. I dragged her to the beach and did CPR on her, but . . ."

"She died?" Victoria finished for him in a small voice. "That quickly?"

"It didn't seem quick."

Victoria shivered. "I'm sure it must have been the most agonizing few minutes of your life."

"It was more agonizing for Kim. I would have done better to just put a bullet in her head—"

"Roan, that's not true, and you know it," Victoria cut in sharply.

"All I know is that I made a stupid mistake, and I should have been the one to die, not an innocent—" He buried his face in his hands, muffling his words. "God, she wasn't much more than a child."

"You didn't do it on purpose. You said it yourself—it was a mistake. An accident. How could you even think it was anything else?"

He balled his hands into fists and slammed them against his knees. "I didn't think, dammit! I ignored her fears of the ocean as if they were nothing. I ignored all the safety rules because I was sure I knew what I was doing. I thought I was so all-fired invincible that no accident would dare intrude into my world."

"But, Roan, we all suffer from bad judgment sometime in our lives. We all have decisions we regret. That doesn't make us bad people."

"Oh, really? When have you ever made a decision that cost someone her life?"

She was silent for a moment, and he thought he'd

made his point. But when she finally answered his question, her words were so soft, he could barely hear them.

"I decided to change my shoes before running out to tell my father the tornado sirens were going off. That two or three minutes could have made the difference."

In the past three years, Roan had never met anyone who could understand what he'd gone through with Kim. He'd listened to their platitudes, shrugged off their comfort, closed his ears when they'd tried to absolve his guilt. He'd been so secure in the knowledge that no one could understand like he did.

Now, here was Victoria Driscoll, telling him that she did understand. She'd been through it. A decision as mundane as what shoes to wear might have cost her her father's life.

When he looked over at her again and their gazes met, he felt a connection to her so strong and powerful, it took his breath away. The magnetic pull was far stronger than even the most insistent sexual desire, more potent than any compulsion he'd ever had. Yet he couldn't close the gap between them, those few inches of cold air that represented a fathomless canyon.

He'd promised, dammit. He'd let her down before, and he would not—

"Roan," Victoria's voice was unsure, like a young girl's. "You don't have to be a gentleman tonight if you don't want to."

He stared at her for several seconds, uncomprehending. Then all at once he understood what she was saying, and the enormity of it scared the hell out of him, almost swamping the red-hot desire coursing through his veins. Almost.

Kissing her seemed too sudden, too radical. He was afraid that if he touched her or tried to hold on to her, she would disappear in a puff of smoke. Instead, he reached out a tentative hand and stroked her hair, all loose and disheveled like he'd never seen it. It was silky soft. And she was real, as real as the porch he was sitting on. More real than any fantasy. Was it just last night he'd dreamed about her hair like this?

She took his hand and pressed the back to her lips in a sweet, gentle gesture that should have touched his heart. Instead, it sent fire to his loins.

"Oh, Vic, what you do to me," he whispered. "But I don't deserve this."

"Don't say that. No matter what you've done, or believe you've done, by simple virtue of the fact that you're human you deserve to be loved."

You deserve to be loved. Did Victoria mean love in the physical sense, or the emotional? Was she telling him how she felt about him, or merely verbalizing a universal truth? And why was he debating semantics when she was offering herself so sweetly?

Already at the limits of his control, he took one look at her moist pink lips, slightly parted, and made a decision he knew could change him forever. He leaned forward and captured those lips with his own, weaving his fingers through her hair as he held her a willing captive.

As before, the kiss was wild and hot, almost painful in its intensity. Unlike before, he felt no compulsion to stop or pull back. She was going to be his. And even if tomorrow she regretted it, he would still have this night and the memory of Victoria's understanding, her willing response, her healing touch.

Her arms stole around his shoulders, her hands like timid birds against the bare skin of his back. Acutely aware of her every breath, every flutter of her eyes, and the soft sounds she made in the back of her throat, he increased the intensity of the kiss, slanting his mouth against hers, invading with his tongue, plundering her sweet recesses.

She melted against him, twisting herself so that her body pressed against his. Her velour robe tickled his chest hair and rubbed against his nipples as she shifted in an effort to bring them closer together.

"Ah, Vic," he groaned against her cheek. She was giving so freely, and all he could think about was taking, taking. He wanted to go slowly, wanted to make it good for her, but she was driving him to the brink of his restraint. And she still had her clothes on.

He yanked on her belt. The robe fell open and his eager hands invaded, circling her waist, then sliding up to cradle her breasts through the T-shirt she wore.

Her sharp intake of breath spurred him on. He stroked her nipples with his thumbs and watched the effects on her expressive face.

"Sh-should we go inside?" she managed to ask.

He nuzzled her neck. "Mmm, you afraid your mama might be watching out the window?"

"No, but it's too cold out here to take off my clothes. And that's what I desperately want to do."

Ah, hell, that she might be cold hadn't even occurred to him. Selfish to the end, always thinking about his own needs first. Well, not tonight, dammit. He would make this the best lovemaking she'd ever experienced.

In one swift move he stood and scooped her into his arms. He kissed the surprised look off her face before carrying her inside, slamming the door with his foot, not stopping until he reached the darkened bedroom.

He set her down and fumbled until he found the switch to the bedside light. A soft illumination filled the room. The double bed was as she'd left it that afternoon, blankets neatly tucked in, the edge of the white eyelet sheet folded back against the blue blanket. With one yank he undid her handiwork. It gave him a supreme sense of satisfaction to know he could now act out the fantasies that had tortured him earlier in this very room.

He would have fallen to the bed and dragged her with him, but the slightly dazed look on her face gave him pause. Slow down, he cautioned himself. He would scare Victoria to death, or more likely disgust her, if he went after her like a stallion in rut.

He ran his hands along the collar of her robe, then framed her face and kissed her as gently as he knew how. Her response was not gentle though. She came alive, all sweet, hot fire. Less tentative this time, she clung to him, her nails biting into his bare shoulders. She rhythmically rubbed the back of his calf with her foot.

He ran his hands along the sides of her neck, insinuating them beneath the robe and scooping it off her shoulders. It fell at their feet, and she kicked it aside with an abandon he wouldn't have thought possible, meeting his bold gaze with one of her own. He made quick work of the sleep shirt, sweeping it over her head, then pausing to feast his eyes on the gentle curve of her waist and the perfection of her breasts, creamy, soft-looking, the rosy tips hardened into pouty peaks. Without conscious thought he dipped his head and took one of her nipples into his mouth.

She gasped and trembled, then moaned as her knees gave way. If he hadn't been holding on to her, she would have fallen.

"Whoa, there," he said, moving her closer to the bed so she could sit down. He was awed by her response to him. "I never made a lady swoon."

She looked up at him with liquid eyes and a tremulous smile. "That's never happened before. It must be sensory overload."

He laughed soft and low. "Honey, we haven't even begun to get overloaded." With that he flicked open the buttons on his jeans, watching her face all the while. Her eyes grew noticeably rounder as he freed his arousal from the confines of clothing. She didn't say a word, but her gaze never left him.

When he'd shucked out of denim and cotton, he waited for her to climb under the covers and make room for him. When she didn't, he realized she was taking all her cues from him. He wondered if she was inexperienced, or just unsure of herself where he was concerned.

He picked her feet off the floor and tucked them beneath the blankets, then walked around to the other side of the bed and climbed in. "You're not scared, are you?"

"A little," she admitted. "Not scared, really, just apprehensive. I haven't had time to get used to the idea, and it's not something I take lightly. . . ."

He laid one hand on her tummy and rubbed slow, sinuous circles. His action silenced her. "Don't be frightened. I would never do anything to hurt you. We'll just take it slow."

Victoria closed her eyes, concentrating on the hypnotic movement of his hand on her abdomen. No simple touch had ever felt so erotic. She would be content to lie there all night and revel in the simple gesture.

But Roan definitely wasn't content with that. He trailed teasing fingertips up and down her arms, her neck, her face. He massaged her breasts, squeezing the nipples between his thumb and forefinger until she thought she would die from the exquisite pressure.

Each time she reached for him, wanting to explore his lean, sinewy body, he stilled her efforts by removing her hand or gently reprimanding her, insisting that she relax and let him pleasure her. She was too weak with wanting to argue.

By the time he slid her panties down her legs, she was an inch away from begging him to take her. She tried to urge him atop her, but he stubbornly resisted, laughing wickedly. "Man, you're hot."

She didn't deny it. She could only hope he wouldn't tease her about it later. She was going against every sensible bone in her body, and she didn't care.

He stroked the brown curls at the apex of her thighs.

"I just don't want to rush things. I want to be sure you're—"

"I'm ready," she said through gritted teeth. She'd been ready fifteen minutes before.

He slid his hand between her legs. She gasped as he parted the petals of her womanhood and teased her with one finger. "So you are."

"Roan . . ." But she realized there was no reasoning with the man. Just as always, he had his own agenda and he wouldn't be swayed from it. Well, fine. For once she couldn't really find fault with his behavior.

"Tell me you want me," he whispered, sliding his finger deeper inside her.

But she was beyond words, and the best she could do was moan his name.

He chuckled again, withdrew his hand, and covered her body with his. "I like the way you say my name," he said between hot, wet kisses. "Your voice turns me on. Always has, from the first words out of your mouth."

She responded by opening herself to him and settling him in the cradle of her thighs. He closed his eyes and grew still, as if savoring the moment of their union. Then he sought the warm haven she offered.

The moment he entered her, her concentration was focused purely on the hot center of her desire. She felt like she'd been hurled from a slingshot into a vast sea of pleasure, and in moments she reached a summit so divine, she thought she would die from it.

She was still reveling in wave after wave of ecstasy when Roan thrust three or four times and cried out, his whole body tensing as he found his release. The moment was so intense, so unexpectedly swift, Victoria was stunned for a few moments. But gradually she floated down to earth. Her breathing slowed, her heart rate returned to something close to normal.

Then she giggled. "See what you get for making me so hot and bothered?"

"I think I made myself more hot and bothered than you. Just be still a minute," he said when she moved her legs to a more comfortable angle. "You're not going anywhere."

"Mmm, I have no intention of leaving."

He kissed her forehead and brushed her damp hair from her face. "You're incredible. So beautiful."

Embarrassed by his praise, Victoria said nothing. But he continued, telling her just how terrific she was in terms that grew more and more explicit. Pretty soon she caught on to his game and joined in, praising his virility, his exquisite skill as a lover. And she wasn't exaggerating one bit. Every sexual encounter she'd had up till then—and there hadn't been that many—seemed bland and featureless compared to this soul-wrenching union with Roan.

He stirred inside her, and she started to object, afraid he was going to pull away. But the stirring turned into a small thrust, then another, and another.

"That's impossible," she whispered.

"Oh, yeah?"

There was no denying that he was fully aroused once again. Victoria closed her eyes and went with it, moving with him, pulling him more deeply into her. Incredible, she thought. Pretty soon she discovered it was possible, for him as well as her. He waited until she tipped over the edge of the universe, and then he joined her.

Victoria had never seen such stamina. By dawn she was exhausted, having made love, dozed, and made love until she'd lost count. Roan had just awakened her again by kissing her stomach and tickling the inside of her thigh.

She was tempted. But Nelva was an early riser, and Victoria would just as soon her mother didn't see her exiting the guest cottage in her nightclothes as the sun came up.

Victoria ruffled Roan's hair. "Come here, you, and kiss me properly."

"Mmm, any way you say," he said in a sleepy voice before obliging her.

She wrapped her arms around his neck and opened herself to the kiss, acknowledging the syrupy warmth that spread through her body. Roan's hand strayed to her breast, but she halted his gentle assault. "One would think you're trying to get in a whole lifetime's worth of sex in one night."

"Maybe I am. Think of all the time we wasted, all those nights we spent in two motel rooms . . ." He kissed her neck and teased her ear with his tongue.

She wiggled and pushed him away. "Roan . . ."

He halted his attempted seduction and looked into her eyes, his face filled with concern. "What's wrong?"

"Nothing, except it's getting late . . ."

He smiled back, reminding her of a mischievous little boy. "Oh. If that's all . . ." He again fondled her breast, and this time she let him. His touch felt so familiar, as if they'd been lovers for years instead of hours.

But she couldn't let him get too carried away. The sky was growing lighter with each passing minute. "Not that this isn't lovely, Roan, but I really do have to go," she said, dredging the words up despite the desire that bloomed inside her yet again. "I don't want Mother to know."

"Why not?" He teased her ear with his tongue. "You're a big girl."

"I'm still a little girl when it comes to my mother." She tried to sit up. "Come on, the coach is about to turn into a pumpkin. It's time for Cinderella to go back to her own castle."

"Is this it, then?" he asked, his voice alarmingly flat and featureless. "Am I back to being a gentleman?"

Victoria smoothed his hair from his face. "You mean, should we go back to being friends and nothing more?" She giggled. "What are you, crazy? You think I'll be able to walk away from the best night of my life and not look back? Don't you have more faith in your seductive powers?" But she chose her next words carefully. "We still have the rest of the trip." Not the rest of our lives.

A smile spread slowly across his face. "Sometimes you surprise the hell out of me, Vic. I was ready for you to turn all proper and insist we forget this ever happened."

"I could never forget. No matter what else—" She cut herself off. "Want to drive into town today?"

He seemed taken aback by the abrupt change of subject. "Sure, I guess. What for?"

"I thought we might visit the drugstore."

"Ohhh. Jeez, babe, I never even thought . . . you mean, you aren't . . ."

She shook her head and shrugged helplessly. "I guess we should have discussed this earlier. If it's any consolation, I have very regular cycles—"

He silenced her with a kiss. "I don't think I want to hear this. Let's not borrow trouble. We'll go to the drugstore."

She found it nearly impossible to pull herself out of the bed, but somehow she managed it. She left Roan stretched out on top of the covers, naked and uninhibited, grinning like a tomcat. *And well he should.*

She'd actually thought about protection earlier, but seeing no way to procure anything at that hour of the night, and unwilling to stop what she'd started, she'd pushed the thought from her mind. It was unlikely she would conceive at this stage of her cycle, but of course there was no guarantee. Oddly, the possibility of her carrying Roan's child wasn't nearly as upsetting as it should have been.

The next three days were the most idyllic Roan could remember. He and Victoria spent their days enjoying farm life and all its simple pleasures. They borrowed two horses from the neighbors and galloped through fallow fields, made homemade ice cream, fed the chickens, and collected eggs. He didn't even mind when Nelva, declaring they should earn their keep, pressed them into service weeding her flower garden.

Thoughts of his sister's death plagued him relatively infrequently now. When he did think about Kim, the pain seemed a little less intense, the guilt less oppressive. He even entertained the possibility that he might deserve forgiveness. Someday. Maybe it was the healing touch of the sun and fresh air and an absence of stress, or maybe it was the fact that Victoria had accepted him warts and all. Whatever the reason, he felt better than he had in a long, long time.

At night Roan waited on the front porch of the guest house for Victoria to come to him. Each time he feared she wouldn't show, that she would change her mind and see the foolhardiness of carrying on with someone like him, a man who couldn't offer her the things she so richly deserved—a permanent home, stability, peace of mind. But each night she came, and they made love until they were too exhausted to move. By their fourth night together, even Roan was willing to admit he'd reached the limits of his sexual prowess. They lay together, sweating and spent, but instead of drifting to sleep as they usually did, Victoria decided she wanted to talk. About them.

It was the moment Roan had been dreading, because he didn't have any answers for her.

"You know, this whole thing has been like a dream," she said. "I don't want to wake up."

"Me neither. But the storms are calling you, right?" She'd been unusually focused on her computer earlier that night, and Roan had guessed that something interesting was going on in the skies.

"The weather is heating up again. Amos won't even give me a clue, but I think Missouri is a good bet for tomorrow. Of course, there's no law that says we have to leave. . . ."

"We can't stay with your mom indefinitely. She's been more than hospitable, but she must be getting pretty sick of us by now. Besides, this is your one chance this year to chase storms, and I don't want to keep you from it. We'll still have nights on the road, right?"

"Yeah. . . ."

He was instantly alert. "You don't sound too sure about that."

"It's just that when we leave here, I'm afraid the spell will be broken. I guess that sounds silly."

"As a matter of fact, it does." He leaned up on one elbow so he could see her clearly. "Victoria, I craved your body before we got here, and I'll still be craving it when we leave. You're not Cinderella, I'm definitely not Prince Charming, and I don't believe in magic spells. I want you in my bed whenever, wherever we happen to be."

"And when the trip's over? That's only a few more days. What happens then?"

He took a deep breath, trying to think of something brilliant and profound to sum up his feelings about that. In the end, he settled for "I don't know."

"I don't either. It would be nice if one of us knew."

"Can't we just see how things go?"

"You mean, maybe we'll be tired of each other by then, and we will have worried for nothing?"

Not in a million years. He didn't think he could ever tire of Victoria, in or out of bed. She challenged and stimulated him in a way no other woman had.

But there were practical reasons why a long-term relationship between them wouldn't work. He had obligations, assignments to be completed. He couldn't drag her around with him to war zones and Amazonian treks even if she were willing, which of course she wouldn't be. She had a job, a career, and it usually didn't take her out of Lubbock, Texas.

He had to admit that for the first time in his life, the concept of a committed relationship didn't seem like a threat. But a tiny aberration in his thinking didn't mean he'd suddenly been given the temperament to stay with one woman the rest of his life. Finding out if he could do it was an appealing proposition, but he had no intention of using Victoria as a test.

He should tell her now that what they had together, no matter how wonderful it felt at the moment, was fleeting. They should simply enjoy it while they could. He needed to learn to live with himself before he could expect someone else to. Admittedly, that goal didn't seem so out of reach anymore. But he was a long way from it.

If he was honest with her up front, she would be prepared for the inevitable parting. And so would he.

But somehow he simply couldn't summon the words he needed. Instead, he held her closer and kissed the end of her nose. "Let's let the future take care of itself, huh? Why waste time worrying, I always say."

"Yeah, I suppose you're right," Victoria said.

No, he was dead wrong. He knew he would spend every waking moment of the next five days worrying, wondering how he would say good-bye to her . . . how he could ever walk away from her.

TEN

Victoria put on a brave face as she closed up the back of the van and said good-bye to her mother. Despite Roan's reassurances, she was worried about how things would go between them once they left the farm. He seemed edgy, and she wondered if he was tired of storm chasing, and maybe a little tired of her. They'd been with each other constantly for over a week.

Now that he'd captured a tornado on film, would he grow bored and antsy to move on to his next adventure? Now that he'd coaxed her into bed and discovered her most intimate secrets, was he ready to move on to his next conquest? Would their time together be reduced to nothing but memories and weather videotapes?

She knew she was being paranoid. Roan had given her no indication that he was in any way bored with her, and he'd made it quite clear he intended their intimacy to continue as long as they remained together.

But they couldn't remain together once her vacation

was over. Perhaps that was what troubled her most of all. During her weakest moments she kept trying to envision a lasting relationship with Roan.

She was spinning impossible dreams, she reminded herself time and again. Despite their obvious sexual compatibility, she and Roan weren't suited to each other. He'd grown up with a father in the military who'd dragged him all over the globe, while she'd been raised on a Nebraska farm. They were at polar opposites when it came to politics; they couldn't agree on movies. He loved to read thrillers, and she thrived on serious biographies. He would never understand her quiet fascination with meteorology, any more than she could relate to his death-defying adventures.

He smoked, for heaven's sake.

Didn't all the experts say that the happiest couples came from similar backgrounds, harbored similar tastes, established similar goals?

Even if she could look past their differences, there was one thing she couldn't overlook: Roan didn't value his own life. One of these days he was going to get himself killed, and she refused to be around when he did.

Dammit, she was not going to let all these depressing thoughts ruin the short time they had left together. This was one storm-chasing trip she would remember the rest of her days. Why mar it by mourning what could never be?

"We're aiming for southeastern Missouri, right?" Roan said, breaking into her thoughts.

She pushed the unpleasant ruminations aside. "Yes.

Ozark country. Not the best terrain for visibility, but we'll have to live with it."

"We'll make better time if we head for Kansas City, then catch 69 South."

Since they had a lot of miles to cover, Victoria agreed to his plan. He'd proven to be a good navigator, as Amos had guessed. She wondered if Amos had any idea just how good his nephew was at a number of skills, like . . .

"Are you going to tell Amos about what's happened between us?" she asked suddenly.

Roan stared at her as if she'd just sprouted horns. "What, are you crazy? If there's one thing in this world that scares me, it's the thought of Uncle Amos with a shotgun aimed at my heart. I plan on dying in a much more exotic way."

"Don't talk like that," she said sharply.

"What? Talk like what?"

"Don't talk so casually about dying."

"It's a joke, Vic."

"I don't like it when you make light of death, especially yours." To her horror, a rush of tears filled her eyes and cascaded down her cheeks. She pulled over to the side of the road and threw the van in park, then fumbled in her purse for a tissue. What was wrong with her?

Ah, hell, she knew what was wrong. She had fallen in love with Roan Cullen.

"Vic?" he said gently, running one finger up and down her sleeve. "Want to tell me what this is about?"

"I don't like to think about people I care for, dying."

"No one does," he said gently. "But everyone has to die sooner or later. And I guess everyone is at least a little bit fearful of that last day on earth. Maybe joking about it is my way of pretending I'm not afraid."

"Are you afraid?"

The seconds ticked by in silence, stretching out until it seemed as if time stood still. Indecision played about his handsome features. At last he answered. "Sometimes. Other times I think about the fact that at least it would end the speculation."

And the pain, she wanted to add, although she knew he was already thinking the same thing. "I don't even care to speculate," she said instead.

Suddenly he smiled. "How did we ever get into such a morbid conversation? Look, I'm sorry if I upset you. The last thing I want to do is hurt you. I'll watch what I say."

Victoria sighed. He just didn't get it. She wasn't worried about her feelings, she was worried about his attitude. She wanted him to value his own life as she valued hers. Maybe in some crazy way she'd believed that she'd given him hope for the future, and that's why his cavalier words about dying had cut her so.

Silly. Did she think he might fall in love with her and magically transform? Did she dare hope she might give him something to live for?

That was exactly what she'd been hoping for, futilely, it seemed.

"I'm okay now," she said, wiping away the last of her tears. "I don't know what's gotten into me. I must be tired . . . or something." She reached for the ignition key, but he grasped her hand and stopped her.

"Vic, look at me."

She couldn't. She was too afraid he would read the truth in her eyes. He tilted her chin up until she had no choice but to meet his gaze. She did so defiantly.

"I'm not planning to clock out anytime soon, okay? Not when I've got nights with you to look forward to. When I'm with you, in bed, I feel safer than anywhere else on earth."

His reassurance was hardly comforting. Sure, she'd given him a reason to live—for the rest of the week. But a man who challenged death on a regular basis would soon grow bored with feeling "safe" in her arms. And after she was gone from his life . . . ?

Since there appeared to be no hope that he could understand her concerns, she pulled up a smile. She felt anything but safe when they made love. She felt open and fragile and far too vulnerable. But she wouldn't tell him any of that.

"I'm just being weird, okay? Let's forget it. Oh, and I agree about Amos. I don't plan to tell him a thing, so you don't have to worry about ducking those shotgun blasts."

They drove hard for several more hours, but the day proved to be a wash.

"I say we hang it up early and buy a bucket of chicken for dinner," she suggested. "This is great country for a picnic."

They were on the northern edge of the Ozark Mountains. The gently rolling hills were awash with wildflowers and the temperature was mild. The puffy white clouds, although not good storm-producers, were pretty as they floated gently past like aimlessly grazing sheep in a field of blue. Victoria was glad that there were no tornadoes that evening. She wanted nothing more than to while away lazy hours with Roan, making daisy chains . . . making love.

Her gaze locked with his, and she knew he'd caught her with her lascivious thoughts. What was worse, she knew he was thinking along the same lines as she, and he wasn't a bit ashamed. She felt her face growing hot with embarrassment as well as desire.

"Chicken sounds good," he said mildly, but his wicked smile told her something else.

A few minutes later they found a roadside diner, which by some miracle featured fried chicken to go. With two box dinners filling the van with a delectable smell, Victoria drove out of town the same way they'd come. She remembered seeing a dirt road that meandered off the highway into a thicket of pine trees—perfect for their picnic.

The road was as she remembered it, a twisting, bumpy dirt path that challenged the van's suspension. She silently apologized to Amos for abusing the Chasemobile.

At last she found the perfect spot, a flat area blanketed in pine needles, overlooking a gurgling creek. The afternoon sun filtered through the trees, covering the area in an ever-changing kaleidoscope of dappled sunlight. She pulled an old blanket from the back of the van and spread it out while Roan fished a couple of not-quite-cold canned drinks from the cooler they'd packed that morning.

Greasy fried chicken and tepid ginger ale. Victoria was stretched out on the blanket, leaning up on one elbow, eating as if this were her last meal, savoring every bite, every moment. And Roan was staring at her as if he wanted to devour her instead of the food.

"Why are you looking at me like that?" she said with a saucy half-smile.

"It's the photographer in me," he said, furrowing his brow thoughtfully. "It's the light and shadow, and the way your hair is mussed up just so . . . stay right there." He abandoned his dinner and went to rummage around in the back of the van.

Great. She'd thought she was inspiring lust, and instead she'd inspired an artistic endeavor.

Soon she discovered that both art and lust were involved. By now she'd gotten used to Roan snapping candid shots of her. But she'd never purposely posed for his photos, and she resisted at first.

"Look into the camera and pretend it's me," Roan coaxed, "and you want to make love to me."

"I do want to make love to you," she said in all seriousness. "But not while you're holding a camera."

He lowered the Nikon and stared at her, licking his lips, and she thought she had him. She unfastened the top two buttons of her blouse and gave him a come-hither look.

"Yeah, that's what I want," he said, quickly bringing the camera up again and snapping off two shots.

"Roan!" She sat up and buttoned her blouse. "Cut that out. I don't intend to take my clothes off for pictures, and that's final."

"Aw, why not?" he asked good-naturedly.

Why not? Because if at some point in the future he started to miss her, she didn't intend for those pictures to take her place. If Roan wanted to see her naked, he would have to come to her and get the real thing.

"I'm just not comfortable acting sexy in front of a camera." She refused to meet his gaze.

He knelt down beside her, his expression full of contrition. "I'm sorry, Vic. You're so uninhibited in bed, I guess I forgot that you're rather, um, conventional in other aspects." He nuzzled her neck. "Come on, we have only a few more minutes of good light. I want to finish up this roll of film—with you fully clothed, don't worry."

Now she felt silly for objecting. She briefly caressed his face, and gave him a light kiss. "How about letting me finish up the film? I'll take pictures of you for a change."

"Sure, okay." He put the camera strap around her neck. "Let's go down by the creek."

They picked their way carefully down a steep incline until they reached the fast-running stream, its waters skipping and dancing over smooth, round rocks, making a pleasing gurgle.

"What do you want me to do?" Roan asked.

"Do? Hmm. Just do what you normally would, I guess."

Her instructions were unnecessary. Roan was already contemplating the creek and the natural bridge of rocks that led to the other side. She laughed as he leapt from stone to stone, hamming it up for the camera, pretending to lose his balance and then catching himself.

She halted mid-laugh as she felt a crawling sensation on her left foot. About the time she looked down and saw the anthill she'd been standing in, the ants began stinging with a vengeance.

She shrieked and, without a second thought, bolted for the creek. The moment she hit the ankle-deep water, she slipped on the mossy bottom. Her legs flew out from under her and she fell with a splash onto her fanny, although she did manage to hold the camera aloft and save it from a fatal dunking.

Still holding the camera up, she pulled off her shoe and rubbed at her sock and the leg of her jeans to make sure the nasty little critters were gone.

"Victoria?" Roan stared at her, balancing on one foot and looking so shocked at her behavior that she would have laughed if she hadn't been so wretchedly cold. "What on earth . . ."

"Antsss," she managed to say, her teeth chattering. She pointed to the shore. "I was s-s-standing in a bed of them."

He immediately came to her, sloshing through the water heedless of getting his own feet wet. He hunkered down so he could see her face, his expression filled with concern. "Did they sting you?"

She nodded. "I don't think it's too bad. The c-cold water is worse. I didn't get your camera wet." She held up the camera triumphantly.

"I wasn't worried about that." He helped her stand on the slippery creek bottom, his expression grim.

Victoria thought his solemn observation an extremely strange one for a man who just hours earlier had been talking so readily about death. It wasn't as if she'd even come close to a serious injury.

He wrapped a protective arm around her waist and helped her back up the creek bank. She couldn't remember ever seeing him so solicitous. Usually when he touched her, there was something sexual going on.

"We've got to get you out of these wet clothes," he said.

She *was* shivering. But his warm hand against her rib cage made her forget about the cold and think instead of fire and dazzling heat. And he wasn't even trying.

He released her to open the back doors of the van, and they dug into their bags for clean, dry clothes. But Victoria found herself distracted by the sight of Roan peeling off his wet jeans. He was unaware of her scrutiny, and she stared at him for several seconds, watching the way those hard muscles rippled beneath his tanned skin.

Suddenly she wasn't a bit cold anymore.

"Roan?"

He looked up. "What?"

She'd forgotten what she wanted to say. Her mouth went dry. She wondered if steam was rising from her skin.

Fortunately, she didn't have to say anything. Roan, as usual, read her perfectly and flashed a lascivious grin. "How quickly do you think we can find a motel?"

"Not quickly enough," she said, taking his damp jeans from him and hanging them over the open van door.

"Oh, Victoria," he said, stretching her name out in that sexy way she loved. He said it that way only when he was feeling romantic. His blue eyes danced with unspoken possibilities. "Right here? I'd think you'd be cold."

"Not a chance," she said, her voice husky.

"Ah." He reached for her, wrapping one hand around her wrist and tugging her to him. "Does that mean you'll warm me up?"

"We'll warm each other up. Isn't that the way it usually works?"

"I don't know, but I'm willing to test your theory." He sat her down on the back bumper of the van and pulled off her soggy tennis shoes and socks, caressing her feet with his warm hands. He then stood her up and started to work on her jeans, but she stopped him.

"I can do this faster on my own," she said, shucking out of the clinging denim. "And I'm not in a mood to waste any time."

"Okay by me." He watched in obvious appreciation as she stripped the rest of the way down, throwing her clothes in all directions. "You really are in a hurry."

"You're not?" she inquired, boldly touching the thrust of his erection through his briefs.

He shut his eyes, savoring her touch for a moment. "Mmm, I didn't say that, sweet wench."

"Then get naked."

"Ma'am, yes, *ma'am*!" He gave her a smart salute before eagerly divesting himself of his T-shirt and briefs. When he was standing gloriously naked before her, his desire for her more than evident, he scooped her into his arms and carried her to the picnic blanket. The sun had sunk behind a hill, but the air was still warm with the memory of afternoon.

Roan stretched out beside her, then covered her body with his. They fit together like two halves of a magnificent whole, and Victoria was struck by a sense of fullness, of completion, that she'd never before encountered.

Everything about him felt right, from his urgent kisses, the passionate, unintelligible words he murmured, his hands, so large and so gentle, overwhelming her small breasts. The moment he took full possession of her was like no other, and she was sure the memory of it would be burned into her brain for eternity.

It wasn't that she was out of control with lust. In fact, this was the first time she could remember approaching their lovemaking with even the semblance of sanity. What struck her, what was so sharp and poignant, was the sense of rightness. She couldn't remember what it was like not to have him inside her, thrusting against her in a perfect rhythm. It was almost as if they were dancing, anticipating each other's moves, reactions. Even their breathing was coordinated.

He was a part of her soul now, and she wasn't afraid for them, at least not for the moment.

They peaked at the same time, as she'd known they would. It was almost as if their minds and hearts were linked instead of just their bodies. Afterward, breathing heavily, he shifted his weight and drew her atop him, then held her close like a drowning man clinging to driftwood.

She kissed his cheek and her heart suddenly constricted. She'd grown so comfortable with him, so used to his virile presence—as if they'd known each other forever. She'd shared more with him than she had with any other man. Her life was going to feel so empty when he moved on. But she had to prepare for that eventuality. He would do what he had to do, and she would let him because she loved him.

He didn't know it, but she'd slipped the roll of film out of his camera and stuck it into her purse. If he could have memories on film, so could she, although they would pale compared to the genuine item.

Making the transition from afterglow to practical matters was difficult. Victoria had a hard time shaking off the sensual mood. But it was getting late and the temperature was dropping. She brushed Roan's cheek with her fingertips, not daring to speak for fear of what might come out of her mouth.

He spoke first. "You're okay, Vic. I mean, incredible."

She struggled for a snappy rejoinder that would ease them back into the teasing banter they'd shared earlier, but none came to mind. "I try," she managed to get out.

The next sizable town likely to have a motel was thirty minutes away. Less than a third of the way there, Victoria's head grew heavy and her eyelids drooped. Darned antihistamines, she thought. She'd taken a couple so the ant bites wouldn't sting as much, forgetting how sleepy they made her.

"Hey, you okay?" Roan asked.

She stifled a yawn. "Mmm, sure." Five more minutes and she pulled over. Much as it pained her, she was going to have to let Roan drive. She reluctantly switched seats with him.

"I don't see what the big deal is," he groused as he pushed back the seat and adjusted the mirrors. "I'm a perfectly good driver. The only wreck I've ever had was Amos's truck, when I was sixteen."

"Then your guardian angel must be working overtime," she said, suddenly not quite so drowsy. "I saw what you did to that rental car."

"That's because I had to take it off-road. I requested a four-wheel drive from Pennywise, but they didn't give me one."

"Well, at any rate, I promised Amos I wouldn't let you drive."

"Ah-hah, I *knew* he'd said something. Talk about holding a grudge!" With that, Roan put the van in gear, put on his blinker, waited for the traffic to clear, and eased out onto the highway.

Victoria kept her eye on the speedometer. Roan

drove at a steady fifty-four miles per hour. In fact, he drove like a little old lady on her way to church.

Amos would never believe this. She wasn't sure she believed it herself. Was it possible she'd actually had an effect on Roan's recklessness? And she noticed he hadn't smoked, at least not around her, for the past couple of days.

Maybe his attitude was changing, she thought, hope blooming in her heart. Of course, he would deny it. But maybe on some deep, subconscious level he was learning to savor life instead of swallowing it whole. And although she didn't expect him to make any radical lifestyle changes because of her, maybe something she'd said or done would make a small difference somewhere, sometime. Perhaps he would remember her and fasten his seat belt, or take some small extra precaution that would save his life.

That thought was comforting. It would be nice to think that something had come out of this trip besides a broken heart.

ELEVEN

"Nothing, nothing, nothing!" Victoria sat on the motel room bed with her long legs curled under her, shuffling through her various maps and charts. Her hair was still damp from her shower, hanging loose and wild the way Roan loved it. She had on one of those prim cotton blouses she was so fond of—pink this time—but she hadn't managed to wiggle into her jeans yet. Roan had to bite his lip to keep from tumbling her across the bed and kissing her until she forgot all about her weather maps and charts.

His need to hold her and keep her close had gotten more insistent by the day, instead of weakening the way it had with other women. He didn't understand it. He'd always been a loner, never needed anyone's company but his own.

Victoria made him think of long evenings by the fire and home-cooked meals. She made him think of babies.

And that terrified him.

For that reason, he deliberately denied the urge he felt to rumple her crisp cotton blouse. He *could* resist her, he told himself. He would miss her when she was gone from his life, but he'd get over it. He had to believe that.

"I've never seen such crummy-looking weather," Victoria said, oblivious of Roan's dark thoughts. She looked up at him with those big hazel eyes and his chest automatically tightened. "I'm afraid that one ropy little tornado may be all we see this trip."

"One is better than none. Cheer up, Vee, we still have three days left."

Her eyebrows flew up. "Vee?"

"Well, you didn't like Vicky or Vic," he reasoned.

She laughed. "Go back to Vic. I was getting used to it. In fact, I was starting to like it."

Roan inhaled sharply. She was flirting with him, giving him that come-hither look, and he was determined he wasn't going to succumb. It was like the cigarettes. He enjoyed them, but he could put them down anytime he wanted. In fact, he realized with a start, he'd gone for several days now without smoking. He'd never gotten around to buying another pack after he'd emptied the last one.

"Are you ready for breakfast?" he asked mildly.

She lowered her gaze and his heart constricted. He'd disappointed her. "Yes, just let me finish getting dressed and do something with my hair."

Victoria hadn't been kidding when she'd bemoaned the state of the weather. The day was as warm and calm and blue-skied as any Roan had seen. Of course, that could always change. But Victoria didn't believe it would, and she wasn't in any particular hurry to get anywhere. Their best bet, she claimed, was to start heading east again and prepare for the new front that would move through Tornado Alley in a couple of days.

They took the van in for an oil change, ate another picnic lunch, then plotted a route on the map that would lead them through some pretty scenery. It would have been a thoroughly pleasant way to spend an afternoon, Roan thought, if leisure had been their goal. But Victoria was clearly impatient with the annoyingly blue sky and gentle breeze, and her edginess was contagious.

He caught himself studying her, imagining in lush detail exactly what he'd do when they stopped for the night, from unbraiding her hair to pulling off her tennis shoes and massaging her feet—and everything in between.

"You're bored," Victoria declared after Roan had unfastened his seat belt, stretched, and tried to find a more comfortable position for the third time in as many minutes.

"I'm not bored," he insisted. He would never be bored around Victoria. Frustrated, maybe. He held back a grin. "Just getting stiff from so many hours in the car. I'm not used to sitting still."

"All right. Since we're in no hurry, let's stop and stretch our legs. Aren't we near some state park?"

Roan consulted the map. "We'll catch Highway 73 in about six miles. If we turn south—"

"Oh, Roan, look at that!"

Roan looked up. Victoria had slowed the van to a

crawl, and he immediately saw what had captured her attention. An old wood-frame church sat in a clearing surrounded by tall pine trees. A single shaft of afternoon sunlight illuminated the glistening white walls and sparkled off the brass bell in the bell tower. Rows of pink and purple tulips lined the stone walkway that led up to the front door.

If it hadn't been for the two cars parked in the lot near the church, Roan would have thought he was witnessing a scene from another time. Automatically he reached behind his seat for his camera bag.

Victoria pulled over. "It's breathtaking, isn't it?" she said in an awed voice. "I say we stretch our legs here. Better scenery than any old state park."

Roan was already out of the van. This quiet church, sheltered in its little grove of trees, evoked a mood he couldn't begin to describe. He had to get it on film.

Worried that the light would change, he didn't bother with a tripod—he just started shooting.

Victoria leaned against the van and watched him quietly as he worked, framing the church first one way and then another, trying different lenses, different light filters. "Will you send me a copy?" she asked.

"Sure. But you have to send me copies from that roll of film you stole out of my camera yesterday."

She laughed, then sobered. "I should have known you'd catch me. But those are the only pictures I've taken of you, and . . . I wanted them. I wanted something to remember you by."

Roan's heart felt as if it were being squeezed in two. Thus far, he and Victoria had avoided talking about their inevitable parting. Somehow, putting it into words made it seem so real . . . so near. He released his camera, letting it dangle from the strap around his neck, and went to Victoria. He wanted to say something, but he didn't know what. Instead, he settled for taking her hand, brushing her knuckles with his lips, then kissing her cheek.

She turned her head and would have kissed him full on the mouth, but he didn't want that. Not that he wasn't about to burst with desire for her. But just this once he wanted her to know that his touching her was more than simple lust. He wanted to communicate his affection, and his genuine appreciation for her presence, body and soul.

She looked at him quizzically, and he smiled. "I hope you will remember me," he said, "and not just as Amos's lunatic nephew who nearly got you killed."

Victoria's eyes grew suspiciously shiny. "You've given me a lot more to remember than that," she said, her voice thick.

He looked away, his own throat feeling uncomfortably tight. "We stopped here to walk, so let's walk," he said gruffly. He still held her hand, and he pulled her roughly along with him as he took off at a brisk pace. He knew he was being stupid, afraid to admit he had emotions, even more afraid to express them.

Wasn't that what men were supposed to do? Brush aside their feelings and head off bravely to slay that next dragon? He looked down at his chest and the slogan on today's T-shirt, which commemorated the most recent California earthquake: I'M ALL SHOOK UP.

That pretty well summed up his current situation.

"Victoria," he said before he could stop himself, "have you given any thought to us seeing each other when we get done with this trip?" He didn't know where the words had come from. He certainly hadn't thought them out. But they came straight from his soul, he realized. For days now he'd been toying with the idea of continuing *something* with Victoria, although until that moment he'd always brushed the idea aside as impossible.

His subconscious must have been chewing on it, though, making decisions without his conscious input.

She didn't answer for a moment, and Roan almost regretted the impulsive query. Maybe she hadn't found their time together as fascinating as he had.

Finally she said, "I thought that was out of the question. I mean, you're globe-trotting all over creation, and I'm stuck working in Lubbock—"

"I'm not on assignment all the time. I do take a few days off every now and then. And there's always the phone, and mail, and fax machines." He couldn't believe he was saying these things. He was actually proposing some sort of continuing . . . relationship. He, Roan Cullen, restless spirit and all-around jerk when it came to women, the man who could pull a disappearing act faster than David Copperfield when any woman tried to get too close, was having a hard time letting go. It boggled his mind.

Again Victoria was slow in answering. "Yes, it's crossed my mind a time or two," she allowed. "We could always try it."

"It might not work," he said.

"It might end up more frustrating than it's worth," she added.

"But you're right, we could try it." He squeezed her hand. That was enough discussion for now. He needed some time to get used to the idea of a relationship. It sounded so . . . settled, so middle-aged, so boring. Then why did it feel so wonderful?

As they came closer to the church, they could hear the sound of children's laughter. Curious, they veered off the country road and walked around to the back of the church. A party of some sort was in progress, judging from the crepe paper and balloons. About a dozen young children and two women were involved in a spirited game of tag.

Instinctively Roan lifted his camera and squeezed off a couple of shots. He wasn't even thinking about where he could sell such a picture. He simply wanted to document the afternoon, the slice in time when he'd reached a crossroads in his thinking about life, about women, about one woman in particular. Now that he knew his time with Victoria wasn't about to end but was only beginning, everything looked different. The air seemed sweeter, the sun warmer, the colors richer. He felt amazingly content.

One of the young women supervising the party had noticed them and walked over, waving and smiling. "Hi, I'm Debbie," she said pleasantly. "Can I help you? Are you lost?"

"No, we're just passing through," Roan answered.

"And we saw the church—it's so beautiful," Victoria added. "We didn't mean to interrupt."

"Oh, nonsense, you're not interrupting," the woman said. "We're just having a birthday party for one of the children in our day care center. Are you a professional photographer?" She pointed toward Roan's camera.

"Yes, ma'am," he said. "Freelance."

"He takes pictures for *Newsweek* and *National Geographic*," Victoria piped in. It gave Roan an unexpected pleasure for her to brag about him.

"Well, then, perhaps you'd like to take some pictures of the birthday boy," the woman said with a mischievous twinkle in her eye. "I forgot my own camera today. I couldn't pay you, but we have lots of ice cream and cake."

Some of the children, most of whom were under five, had wandered over to listen to the exchange, and they immediately took up a chorus of "Take my picture! Take my picture!"

"Sure, why not?" Roan replied. He popped a fresh roll of film into his camera and began taking shots of the kids, making sure he included all of them, even the shy ones. He shot the whole roll, then took it out and handed it to Debbie. "Now, where's my payment? I hope the cake's chocolate." He already knew it was.

Debbie cut him a generous slice and topped it with a mountain of vanilla ice cream. He sat down in a metal folding chair next to Victoria, who was already working on her dessert, and dug in.

"That was nice of you," she said.

"Nice, hell. I was hungry. I've been a freelancer long

enough to know not to turn down any paying assignment."

When he'd eaten as much of the cake as he could manage, he set his plate aside and wandered over to the edge of the clearing to peer through the trees at the sky. A peculiar darkness hovered just above the horizon. It was probably just an optical illusion, a trick caused by heat and atmosphere, but he thought enough of it to motion Victoria over to have a look.

"Hmm" was all she said.

"Don't you think we should check it out?"

"Well, it couldn't possibly be anything of consequence," she reasoned. "There hasn't been anything in the data all day to indicate storms, or even precipitation."

Roan wasn't as trusting of the data as Victoria. "Let's go have a look anyway." Hell, at least it gave them something to do. They bade good-bye to the birthday party and returned to the van. Roan navigated them toward the mysteriously dark horizon, and the chase was on.

"It couldn't be anything," Victoria said more than once as she fiddled with the ham radio, searching for some kind of verification for what her eyes told her.

"Well, it looks like something," Roan said. And the closer they got to it, the more ominous it became. Before long, there could be no denying the cumulus cloud formations—tall, crisply defined towers exploding right before their eyes. High winds sheared off the tops of the clouds, forming a classic "anvil." Roan hadn't even begun to scratch the surface of Victoria's knowledge of severe weather, but he did remember her telling him that such a cloud was a good indicator of possible tornadoes.

"It's a supercell," she finally declared. "A classic tornadic supercell. But it can't be! There's been no indication. No one's talking about it on any frequency. I mean, something like that has to be showing up on radar!" As they topped a hill, she pulled over onto the shoulder. "We can watch from here. I'm going to pull up some new data."

"I don't see why you'd want data now," Roan said. "I mean, why would you need to verify what's in the sky right in front of you?"

"But there has to be some indication, some warning," she muttered, ignoring him. "Something I've missed."

Roan climbed out of the van and began setting up his videocamera on a tripod. If Victoria wanted to play with her computer while this drama was going on, that was her loss. He intended to capture it on film, whatever "it" turned out to be. The wind had picked up, and the clouds churned wildly. The sky was as black as he'd ever seen it, tinged with green—another forewarning that this was no ordinary storm.

When he spotted a wall cloud—a rotating wagon-wheel formation that dropped from the base of the storm—he knew something spectacular was about to happen. Victoria had taught him about wall clouds.

He leaned inside the open door of the van. "Vic, you'd better come look at this. I think we're about to have a tornado."

"That's impossible," she said, peering at the map that the computer printer was spitting out. "There's absolutely no way a tornado could form under these conditions."

"Far be it from me to dispute your data," he said, his sarcasm evident, "but would you please come look at this?"

"Just a second. I want to check one other thing." She began punching various buttons on the computer keyboard.

Roan threw up his hands. The woman was in denial. Well, just because she wanted to insulate herself with her computer analysis, that didn't mean he had to miss the best atmospheric display he'd ever seen. He checked his video camera to be sure it was recording the show, then began snapping off stills with his Nikon. Lightning flashed in neon forks, arcing from cloud to cloud, and sometimes hitting the ground. The accompanying thunder rumbled menacingly.

Then he saw it. His heart was in his throat as the wall cloud produced an ominous, twisting tendril that reached for the earth like a rope being dangled before a playful cat. Soon a second twister joined the first, and then a third. They circled around each other in a macabre dance, kicking up dust in their wake, eventually merging and blending until they formed one hellacious-looking tornado.

Roan was fascinated with the dynamics. This tornado was obviously not like the other one. It was bigger, more powerful, scarier. But it was also a good distance away. He didn't think they were in any danger, not yet.

He didn't want to be an alarmist, but he wouldn't make the same mistake as last time. He might be awed by the twister, but not so overwhelmed that he wasn't going to get the hell out of the way long before he put anyone's life in peril, including his own.

The tornado changed in shape and color as it worked its way closer to them. It began as a thin gray column, but as it picked up debris that fueled it, it thickened into a fat wedge and darkened until it looked like the sooty smoke from a raging fire.

When he could actually hear the tornado's roar and feel the sting of dust in the wind, Roan judged he'd waited long enough. He quickly packed up his gear and threw it into the back of the van, then checked on Victoria again. She was on the cellular phone, arguing with someone about the fact that no tornado watch had been issued. At the same time, she was shuffling wildly through her stack of maps, apparently still searching for that elusive clue she'd missed.

Now, finally, Roan had all the pieces of the puzzle that was Victoria. With her radios and her fancy analysis program, she thought she had some degree of control over the weather. The more she understood, the more accurate her forecasts, the more confident she'd felt that nothing could take her by surprise—as the tornado of her childhood had.

Now she simply couldn't face the unhappy truth that wind and rain didn't always follow man's rules.

Knowing he had to get her attention, and fast, Roan plucked the phone out of her hand and hung it up.

"What are you—" she objected.

He grabbed the stack of computer printouts. "Lady, I don't give a damn what your data say, you can't argue with this!" He flung the papers out the door, where the wind whipped them up into the air and scattered them like confetti.

"Roan, have you lost your mind?"

He circled her arm with his hand and yanked her out of her chair, then out of the van.

She stumbled and he caught her. "Roan . . ." She started to object, but then she saw it. Her face turned the color of oatmeal and her eyes were as big and round as saucers as she stared at the massive, churning wedge of destruction that was now much too close for comfort. "Oh, my God . . ."

Roan didn't wait for anything more. He shoved her back into the van, slid the side door closed with a slam, and raced around to climb into the driver's seat. She would probably be furious with him for treating her so roughly, but just then all he cared about was getting them the hell out of there—out of danger.

Thank God she'd left the keys in the ignition. Not bothering with the seat belt, he gunned the engine to life and roared into a sharp U-turn.

In moments Victoria leaned across the console between the two front seats. "Where are you going?"

"Away from that thing," he said, gesturing with his thumb. "You're the expert. Which way is it going, and how do I get as far away from it as possible?" He knew he sounded gruff and angry, but better that than revealing how he really felt—scared. What if he'd waited too long to alert Victoria to the danger?

What if they both got killed, just when they were on the brink of stumbling into this fantastic relationship thing?

The fear—not just for Victoria's life, but for his own, and for their future—was a new feeling for him, or perhaps only one he'd forgotten. Suddenly he felt intensely alive, like he hadn't in years.

And he wanted to stay that way. Badly.

He came to a crossroads. "Which way, Victoria?" he demanded.

"Right." He started to turn, but she laid a hand on his shoulder. "No, wait. The church!"

"What?"

"The tornado is heading straight toward that church. I don't hear any sirens." She gripped his shoulder, her fingers digging painfully into his flesh. "They weren't listening to a radio. They won't have any warning, and they won't see it coming with all those trees around. Oh, Roan, all those children! They'll be so frightened. We have to warn them."

Roan thought it exceedingly unlikely that the storm would hit the church. They were several miles away from it now, and it seemed a strange thing to turn directly into the path of the deadly storm, when his newly rediscovered survival instinct told him to run like hell. But there was no way he could worry about saving his own butt and leave a churchyard full of children in danger, no matter how remote the danger was.

With a sinking feeling, he turned left.

TWELVE

Victoria climbed over the console and into the passenger seat. The shock of seeing that giant tornado bearing down on them was fading, replaced by a sense of panic. What had come over her? She'd been so absorbed by the fact that the weather wasn't behaving predictably, so obsessed with finding some warning sign in the data, she'd ignored the threat of danger. She'd been more willing to trust computer printouts and radar reports than what she saw with her own eyes!

And she hadn't trusted Roan's warnings at all. Was it only days before that she'd nearly chewed him to dust for not paying attention to *her* warnings?

"I'm sorry, Roan," she said. "I got crazy there for a minute, but I'm okay now."

His gaze never left the road, but he reached over and squeezed her hand. "It's all right, Vic. I know what it's like to be a little . . . single-minded."

He was being too kind, but she appreciated it.

"My God, would you look at that thing?" She almost whispered the words in reverence. The surrounding trees obscured her visibility, but every so often she caught a glimpse of the tornado annihilating everything in its path.

"I'm trying not to look at it. Is it gaining on us?"

"No, we're outrunning it. I don't think it's moving very fast. At least we're ahead of the rain and hail."

Finally she heard some bewildered-sounding storm spotters reporting the tornado on ham radio. The Weather Service quickly issued a warning. Victoria picked up the microphone and dutifully made a report.

She watched the tornado out her window when she could. And when the road turned and the twister was no longer in view, she watched Roan. He was driving fast, his jaw clenched in concentration. Was he enjoying this drama a bit too much? she wondered. But no, he didn't appear to be enjoying it at all. The road turned again, and they were once again driving into the path of the storm.

"How far do you think we are from the church?" she asked, seeking reassurance. This was probably the most foolhardy thing she'd ever done. But if anything happened to those children, she could never live with herself. She suspected Roan felt the same way.

"Too far," he replied.

"You're not wearing your seat belt," she scolded.

"Neither are you."

"What? Oh, you're right." They both clicked their safety belts into place.

Victoria breathed a sigh of relief when the church's

white steeple came into view. As Roan screeched into the parking lot, the teachers were starting to herd the children inside. Just as Victoria had predicted, they could not see the storm from there. The only warning signs they had were a darkening sky overhead and a moderately brisk wind.

Victoria jumped out of the van and ran toward Debbie, who looked surprised to see them again.

"Did you forget something?" she asked pleasantly.

"Do you have a storm shelter?" Victoria demanded. "Or a basement? There's a huge tornado headed this way."

Debbie appeared confused. "But surely the sirens would—"

"Please!" Victoria cried. "I've just seen it. It's only a few miles away and it's coming this direction. We have to get everyone to shelter."

"The church doesn't have a basement," Debbie said, "but there's a shelter—Martha!" She called to the other teacher and, when she had her attention, quickly related the news.

Martha, who was even younger than Debbie, burst into hysterical tears.

"Oh, hell," Roan said. "Debbie, where's the shelter?"

"It's over there," she said, pointing to the other side of the church. "But I don't think it's been open in years. Couldn't we just take shelter in the church?"

"No," Victoria said at once. "This is an F-5 or F-6 tornado," she said, then, realizing the scale would mean nothing to a layperson, added, "It's a killer, and a wooden church with all those windows would be worse than nothing." Even as she spoke, rain began to fall in big, hard drops.

"Come on, kids," Roan said, trying to round up the children, who were wandering around like restless sheep. "We're going to play hide-and-seek, and I know just the place to hide."

Most of the children responded immediately to him, following obediently. They didn't know enough to be frightened. Victoria picked up two of the littler ones who were lagging behind, while Debbie took the hysterical Martha by the hand.

The double doors to the storm shelter were set at a forty-five-degree angle into the side of a hillock. Roan flung them open, and a musty smell escaped. Concrete steps led down to blackness.

"I'll go first," Debbie volunteered. Some of the older, more adventurous children followed right behind her, but the rest balked and some of them began to cry. It became a test of wills to get them all inside the shelter, which was dark as a crypt and twice as scary. Martha was worse than some of the children, and Victoria had to threaten her with bodily harm before she would go down the stairs.

Victoria followed, descended four steps, then waited for Roan, in case he needed help with the doors.

He didn't come.

She turned to look back questioningly at him. Their gazes locked long and hard.

"Stay put," he said. "I'll be back." He remained outside, closing the shelter doors and plunging her and the others into blackness.

Pandemonium reigned inside the shelter as Debbie attempted to get a head count of the children, no small task when half of them were crying and no one could see. Martha had calmed somewhat and was trying to help.

But Victoria felt removed from the situation, insulated by a cocoon of raw pain. How could Roan have so little respect for his own life that he would deliberately stand in the path of a killer tornado? But why else would he have denied himself the safety of this shelter? She remembered those videotapes where he'd stood out on a beach in the midst of a hurricane, opening his arms wide to the wind, exultant, excited by the storm's violence.

A few minutes ago, when he'd been so set on getting them out of danger, she'd thought things were different, that he'd learned—that she'd taught him—to value his own life. But obviously the concern he'd shown had been for her life, not his. Now that she was stashed in a safe place, he was just as determined as always to throw himself into peril.

He hadn't changed. He still had a death wish. And she couldn't, wouldn't, remain involved with a man who was set on self-destruction. She would have to break things off with him immediately. The longer she delayed, the more painful it would be. She would tell him the minute she saw him again.

If she saw him again.

She brushed an errant tear off her cheek with the back of her hand. Telling Roan good-bye would be the hardest thing she'd ever done; not being able to tell him would be much, much worse. He could so easily be killed.

The storm outside intensified until the roar of the wind sounded like a laboring freight train. Debbie had given up trying to count the children and had simply gathered as many of them around her as she could, holding them tightly against her.

Two warm little bodies clung to Victoria's legs. She leaned down and hugged them close. "We'll be okay," she said, though she doubted they could understand her above the noise. Hail bombarded the storm-shelter doors, cracking like gunfire against the wood, which started the children crying again.

The assault seemed to last forever, though it was probably only three or four minutes. Then the roar abated, the hail turned to pattering rain, and the storm retreated abruptly. The sudden quiet was eerie.

"When can we leave the shelter?" Debbie asked, deferring to Victoria's authority.

Victoria took a deep breath. "I'll have a look outside. Sometimes these things come in twos and threes . . . but it sounds as if the worst is over."

Debbie reached out across the darkness and touched Victoria's arm. "Your friend . . . why did he stay outside?"

Because my love wasn't enough to save him? Victoria's voice cracked when she answered. "I don't know. I just don't know."

She felt her way up the steps and heaved the doors open. All was quiet. Even the rain had stopped. She poked her head out, then stepped outside. "Oh, dear God."

The destruction was so vast as to be almost incomprehensible. Trees were uprooted, cars overturned, and debris slung everywhere—planks of wood ripped from buildings three counties away, probably. She identified telephone poles, twisted bits of metal that were once road signs, a garbage can, a stray shutter, bricks, a dead bird.

She was afraid to turn and look at the church. When she did, she breathed a sigh of relief. It was missing a few shingles from the roof, and one of the stained-glass windows was broken, but it was largely intact. And it was about the only thing left standing.

"Your friend probably took shelter in the church," Debbie said. She'd emerged from the storm cellar behind Victoria, and was taking in the devastation with a grim face.

"Yes, I'm sure he did," Victoria replied, though she wasn't at all sure. "Let's take the children inside, away from all this debris where they could get hurt."

Even as she helped herd the children toward the church, Victoria scanned the landscape for some sign of Roan. He could be anywhere. He could be in Oz.

A little boy of six or seven—the birthday boy, she realized—grabbed hold of her hand. His face was pale, his eyes huge. "Come this way."

"But we have to go into the—"

"No, come this way. It's Mr. Roan. He's hurt."

Oh, no. Oh, please, God, no. She let the little boy lead her across the debris-strewn yard, skirting a wad of barbed wire, climbing over a white picket fence that was miraculously still upright.

He directed her toward a stand of trees. She gasped when she saw Roan, stretched out prone on the ground, all but covered by a huge tree limb that had fallen on top of him.

Victoria had never moved so fast. She heaved the limb off Roan, though it probably weighed more than a hundred pounds. "Roan?" she said, kneeling beside him, feeling around his neck for a pulse.

One of his hands twitched, and she knew he was alive, at least.

The little boy, all but forgotten by Victoria, started to sniffle. "I didn't mean for nobody to get hurt," he said.

Victoria knew the child was frightened, but she couldn't spare him much in the way of comfort or sympathy. She had to direct all her energy to Roan. What she did in the next few moments might mean the difference between life and death.

She wished she knew the boy's name. "Run back to the church and ask your teacher to call for an ambulance. Can you do that?"

"No ambulance," came Roan's muffled objection.

Oh, thank God. "Roan, don't try to move," she cautioned. "You could be badly injured—"

As she might have expected, he ignored her warning and pushed himself up on his elbows, then his hands and knees, and finally into a sitting position.

"Roan, you shouldn't—"

"I'm okay," he said, rubbing the back of his head.

Then he looked up, noticing the chaotic state of the churchyard for the first time. "Holy . . . was anyone else hurt?"

"Everyone else was in the storm shelter, where you should have been," she replied curtly. "Now you probably have a concussion and who knows what else."

He looked up at her and flashed that roguish half-smile that had always made her knees go weak. "Well, aren't you Little Mary Sunshine. How about some TLC for the wounded?"

She wanted to give in to his charm. Every nurturing bone in her body urged her to touch him, soothe his obvious pain. But she'd made a decision, and she was going to stick with it. The sooner he understood how things were going to be, the better.

"I'm sure they must have a first aid kit at the church," she said briskly. "Can you stand up?" She offered her hand for support. He was a little shaky, but he made it to his feet. She immediately released his hand.

He reached up and touched the camera that was still hanging from his neck by a leather strap. It was smashed almost beyond recognition. "Oh, damm—ah, darn," he said, since the birthday boy was still standing there, watching Roan intently. "That was my favorite camera too, my old Nikon."

Victoria picked off a weed that was clinging to the camera. "I sure hope the pictures were worth it," she said frostily before turning and stalking back toward the church, leaving Roan to his own devices. She was torn between anger and grief for the love they'd so recently discovered, for the relationship that might have been. Right now it was easier to hide behind the anger.

Roan couldn't blame Victoria for what she was no doubt thinking. She obviously didn't understand why he'd chosen to remain outside the shelter. She'd automatically assumed that he would blithely throw himself into danger for the sake of a photograph, for the sake of a thrill. She hadn't even asked him to explain.

The fact that she'd jumped to the wrong conclusion crushed him, worse than that tree branch had.

Ah, hell, he had no right to expect her to trust him or believe in him. After all, what had he done to deserve her faith, to prove he'd changed? He'd quit smoking, and for all he knew, she hadn't even noticed. He'd tried like hell to get them away from the tornado when she would have sat there all day punching numbers into a computer.

He'd talked about a future with her.

But, of course, she had no way of knowing what a departure from the norm that had been.

Now the question was, could he set things right again? Or was it possible that Victoria would never believe in his sincere desire to have a future with her, a long future? A forever kind of future?

"Are you really okay?" the little boy asked in a small voice.

"Sure. Just a little bump on the head." He rubbed the back of his throbbing head again, gingerly probing the knot that had formed. "How 'bout you? I didn't hurt you when I fell on you, did I?"

The boy inspected a minor scrape on his elbow.

"I'm okay. I'm really sorry, Mr. Roan. I didn't mean for you to get hurt. It's just that I never seen a t'nado before."

He wanted to let the kid off the hook. In the boy, Roan saw himself at that age, always getting into trouble, climbing things he shouldn't, taking chances, sometimes getting hurt in the process, though never seriously. But he gritted his teeth and said what needed to be said.

"You disobeyed your teacher, and you could have easily been killed. Not only that, you could have gotten someone else killed, namely me. And trust me, that's something you don't want on your conscience the rest of your life."

The boy's eyes filled with tears. "Okay. I won't do it again, I promise. Next time Miss Debbie or Miss Martha tells me to go somewhere, I'll go."

That was good enough for Roan. The kid would probably catch hell from his teachers anyway. He ruffled the boy's dark hair. "All right. Think you could tell me where to find some ice, and maybe a couple of aspirin? I've got a heckuva headache."

The kid smiled up at Roan with a look of pure adoration. "Sure, no problem." He grabbed Roan's hand, and they headed back to the church.

When Roan limped into the church, he was immediately surrounded by the children and the two teachers, who lavished attention on him. Was he hurt? Did he need to sit down? What was it like out in the tornado?

Victoria couldn't stomach it, so she went outside through a side door. No wonder Roan was such a daredevil, if that was the kind of treatment he was used to. He got a lot of positive reinforcement for his death-defying nonsense.

Well, not from her.

The cars in the parking lot were a sorry sight, pocked by hail, windows broken. Victoria had seen worse. She'd once seen a tornado pick up a truck and hurl it several hundred feet. But that still didn't prepare her for the sight of the Chasemobile—which was not exactly where Roan had parked it.

She walked around what was left of Amos's cherished van. How in the world was she going to explain this? One side of the vehicle was completely caved in, the window glass shattered. The computer and printer had obviously been tossed around like dice in a cup. They lay smashed and useless in a back corner of the van. And everything that wasn't smashed was soaking wet.

Amos was going to kill her!

She sighed. Amos would do no such thing. His only concern would be for the safety of the van's occupants. But it was easier to worry about Amos than to think about Roan.

"Ma'am?"

Victoria turned. It was the birthday boy again. "What are you doing out here?"

"I have to tell ya something."

Although she wasn't in the mood for little boys' games, she forced herself to be patient. "Yes, what is it?"

"It's about Mr. Roan." The boy lowered his voice to a reverent whisper. "He saved my life."

"Now, how do you figure that?" she asked. If this was some trick, some feeble attempt by Roan to get back into her good graces, it was going to backfire—big-time. He might think himself a big, brave, macho kind of guy, but to have a cute little boy plead his case for him was worse than cowardly.

"When you said there was a t'nado coming, I ran and hid behind a tree," the boy explained earnestly. "I didn't want to go in that old shelter. I wanted to stay outside and see the storm."

Victoria felt a niggling doubt creep into her mind. The boy's story had the ring of truth to it. And, come to think of it, she didn't specifically remember ushering him into the shelter or hearing his voice in there. She didn't remember Debbie or Martha speaking to him.

"But Mr. Roan saw where I'd hid, and he came to get me," the boy continued. "But by then it was too late, and the t'nado was right there, and the trees were blowing all the way to the ground. Mr. Roan threw me down and fell on top of me. And then the tree fell on us, and I didn't know what to do, so I just stayed there until it was all over." He paused to wipe away tears with one grubby hand. "I thought Mr. Roan was dead 'cause he didn't move. So I crawled out, and that's when I came to get you."

Victoria was stunned to silence. She would never in a million years have guessed the true story behind the risk Roan had taken. To stand out in a tornado because he wanted to take pictures was one thing. But to try and save a little boy's life . . . !

"Are you mad at me?" the repentant child asked, wiping his eyes with the back of his hand.

She leaned down and gave him a hug. "No, honey, I'm not mad. Thank you for telling me."

"Are you mad at Mr. Roan?"

She straightened, giving him one last pat on the shoulder. "No, I'm not mad at anyone."

"Chris!" Debbie stood in the church doorway, her hands on her hips. "Christopher Walker, you get your . . . you get in here right now!"

"Yes, ma'am!" He took off at a run.

Victoria hugged herself. She'd really messed things up by automatically thinking the worst of Roan. How was she ever going to make it up to him?

She all but ran back to the church herself, eager to see him again, touch him, hold him, reassure herself that he was really all right. And then she was going to get him someplace private, and throw herself on his mercy.

Roan was surprised Victoria was able to start the van, much less that it went anywhere. They had said their good-byes to the church group. Fire trucks and other emergency vehicles were starting to flock to the area, apparently the hardest hit by the tornado. And that meant television news crews weren't far behind. Roan, at least, wanted to get the heck out of there before the reporters arrived. He didn't want any accolades for his act of heroism. No one had to know what he'd done. There was only one person whose opinion mattered to him—and the jury was still out.

He had to face the fact that Victoria might never forgive him for staying outside in the storm, even if she understood why he'd done it. He'd risked his life for a noble cause, but he'd risked it all the same.

Victoria liked things predictably safe, and he wasn't sure she could ever deal with someone like him on a long-term basis. True, she had helped him to put some things into perspective, but he would never be the kind of man who always played it safe.

"How's your head feeling?" Victoria asked as she aimed the limping van out of the parking lot.

"Not bad." Not as bad as his heart. "Victoria . . ."

"Roan . . ." she said at the same time. They both laughed self-consciously. "Roan," she tried again. "Why didn't you tell me why you were staying out in the storm? I could have helped you find Chris and bring him back to the shelter."

"That's exactly why I didn't say anything. I didn't want to panic Debbie and Martha by pointing out that he was missing, and I certainly didn't want you outside with me. I knew right where he was hiding. All I had to do was run over, grab him, and bring him back. I wasn't counting on getting knocked flat by a flying tree branch."

"Then why didn't you explain when I found you?"

"You didn't exactly ask for explanations."

Victoria was silent for a few moments. She bit her lip, apparently concentrating on her driving. They were coming into the little town of Marshall, where Debbie had said there was a motel. "No, I didn't ask you to explain. I thought I knew exactly what had happened. And I was so damned hurt and disappointed . . . well, maybe I wanted to hurt you back."

"You succeeded," he said simply.

She pulled into the first parking lot they came to, and just in time. The van's engine stalled and died. She didn't even try to start it again. "I'm sorry," she said, her voice clogged with tears. "I'm so sorry."

He didn't know if she was apologizing for hurting him, or for the fact that things weren't going to work out between them. Either way, he couldn't stand to see her so upset. He reached over and stroked her cheek. "Please don't cry, Vic. I'm not worth it."

Her eyes opened wide and the tears receded. "Not worth it? Not worth it? How can you say that? You risked your life to save a little boy. Roan Cullen, you're the most—"

"Exasperating?"

"That too, but I was going to say you're the most worthy man I know."

"But not the man for you," he concluded.

"Why do you say that?"

Roan took a deep breath. Could it be he was the one jumping to incorrect conclusions? "I just thought you'd probably decided you couldn't handle me taking the risks I do, good reason or no."

"That's not at *all* what I decided." She stared at him, long and hard, and then she took his hand. "But I did reach some significant conclusions today. Do you want to know what they are?"

He nodded, not trusting himself to speak.

"First, I learned that no matter how carefully you plan, life can still throw you a curve. And I'm not just talking about the weather."

He nodded again, agreeing with her. "Go on. What else did you learn?"

"I learned to have more faith in the man I love."

His breath caught in his throat. "Did you just say . . ."

"Oh, yeah, I skipped one. I learned that I'm deeply, irrevocably, in love with you, Roan Cullen. And I don't have any idea whether you love me back, whether you even want anything to do with me after I was so ready to condemn you for something you didn't do. But sometimes you have to take risks. So I'm taking one. Because I couldn't stand another minute of not telling you how I feel." She stared at him defiantly, waiting for him to respond. And looking like she expected to be shot down.

"Victoria." He said it slowly, stretching out every syllable, because her name had become so dear to him, he hated to let it go. He pulled her close and kissed her, softly at first, then more insistently. He buried his face against her hair and, for a moment, just listened to their tandem breathing.

"I've learned a couple of things too," he finally said. "Want to hear them?"

"Yes, very much," she answered breathlessly.

"First off, I'm an adventurous man, and I'll never be otherwise. Wait, wait, let me finish," he said when she started to object. "I like to travel, see new sights, experience new things. But there's no thrill in the world—not volcanoes or hurricanes or skydiving, or even a mile-wide tornado flying right over me—that compares to the thrill of loving you."

"Oh, Roan—"

"I do love you, Vic," he said, unwilling to let her interrupt him. He had to get everything out in the open now. "And I want you in my life—now, next week, forever. If that means I have to take a nine-to-five job shooting video for a TV station or . . . or working at the Sears Portrait Studio, I'll do it. Whatever it takes to stay inside your comfort zone, I'll do it. I don't want to lose you. I want to marry you."

Tears spilled out of her eyes and rolled down her cheeks.

He cupped her face in his hands, forcing her to look at him. "Is that 'yes' crying, or 'no' crying?"

"Y-yes," she managed to say. "But, Roan, I don't want you to work at some boring nine-to-five job. You could never be happy, and I wouldn't be happy knowing I'd caged you. I want you to continue your freelancing. It's part of what makes you who you are, part of what made me fall in love with you."

"Against your better judgment," he added.

She laughed, hiccuped, brushed aside her tears with an impatient swipe.

"Regardless, I intend to scale down my exploits," he said. "No more climbing into volcano craters, or jumping canyons with motorcycles—"

"Oh, dear God, please tell me you haven't tried that too!"

He cleared his throat and averted his gaze. "The point is, I won't be doing it again. Because now I'll have a reason to stay whole and healthy. I'll have someone to come home to, maybe even a couple of someones. You want children?" He realized there were still a lot of things he didn't know about Victoria. But he intended to have the adventure of his life learning about her.

"A house full of them," she replied, leaning closer to kiss him again . . . and again.

"Mmm, perhaps we should continue this discussion elsewhere?" he suggested.

She sighed. "Only if I can get the van started again."

He shook his head. "Not necessary. The Chase-mobile died in a very opportune location." He pointed out the window to the sign on the closest building: THE DROP-IN MOTOR LODGE. "Romantic, huh? And it even has cable TV."

Victoria pulled reluctantly out of his embrace and heaved open her door, which now had a tendency to stick. "Roan, the last thing I want to do right now, and for quite some time, is to watch the Weather Channel."

He grinned wickedly. "Me neither. I'll do my own forecast. I predict some heated kisses and stormy love-making, followed by warm afterglow . . . and maybe a pizza in bed."

Victoria blushed, but she didn't contradict him.

EPILOGUE

The tow truck pulled into Amos's driveway, dragging the crippled Chasemobile behind it. Roan had gotten the van started again, and it had lasted a couple of days, but it had finally given up for good just inside the Texas border.

"Oh, heaven help us, there he is," Victoria said from the front seat of the tow truck, where she sat between Roan and the driver. Amos had just come out the front door onto the porch. Neither she nor Roan had worked up the nerve to tell Amos about his van when they'd talked to him on the phone. They'd decided to deliver the news in person, and to couple it with a piece of really good news, so Amos wouldn't be so crushed.

They got out of the truck. Amos came toward them, silent, his expression betraying nothing. He walked all the way around the van as the tow truck driver unhitched it. Victoria groped for Roan's hand, found it, squeezed it.

Finally Amos stopped, folded his arms, and treated Victoria to a penetrating stare. "I told you not to let Roan drive."

Victoria couldn't help it—she started laughing. "Oh, Professor, if you only knew! Roan wasn't driving when all this happened. In fact, no one was near it. This is what the Marshall, Missouri, tornado did to the van while it was sitting in a parking lot."

Amos's face paled, and he examined the van more closely. "A tornado did this, huh? Sheesh. Maybe it's time for me to get out of the storm-chasing business." He waved an accusing finger at his nephew and his protégé. "Where were you two when this was going on? You told me you'd caught the Marshall tornado, but just exactly how close did you get to it?"

"A little too close for comfort," Roan said, all but shuffling his feet.

"Dammit, Roan, I told you to listen to Victoria and she'd keep you out of trouble. But you didn't." He spared one more look at the van. "No, I can see that."

"Wait a minute, Amos," Victoria said. "This wasn't Roan's fault. I was the one who didn't know when to tuck tail and run. Even then, we would have made it out of the way in plenty of time, except there was this church, and all these children . . ."

Amos's outrage ran out of steam at the mention of children. "Oh, no matter," he said. "The important thing is that you're both all right. And getting along all right too, it seems." His gaze locked onto their clasped hands.

"We're doing more than getting along," Victoria

said, but she was suddenly nervous about springing their other surprise on an unsuspecting Amos. Would he really be happy about it?

"We got married," Roan blurted out.

Amos's mouth hung open, and then he said, "You're joking, right?"

Victoria shook her head and held out her left hand for Amos's inspection. Three days after the tornado, she and Roan had wed in the little white church that had symbolized a turning point in their lives.

"Well, I'll be dipped," Amos said. "Married? You two? I mean, I knew there was some chemistry going on, and I figured if you were forced to spend two weeks together you'd start to appreciate each other, but I never imagined . . . Sounds like y'all have a heckuva story to tell me." He smiled, and Victoria relaxed.

"Now, Professor, you don't honestly expect us to tell you the whole story, do you?"

"Just the parts that aren't X-rated," he said with a wink.

Victoria paid the tow truck driver, then followed the two men into the house. Roan was already bending Amos's ear with tales of the road trip, using his flair for the dramatic to make a harrowing story sound even more exciting.

Still, he was so much more relaxed than he'd been two weeks before. He seemed to finally be at peace with himself and the world. And Victoria felt a new measure of peace herself. She no longer harbored that frantic need for her domain to be so perfectly predictable.

She sat down on the couch next to Roan and rested her hand possessively on his knee. He was anything but predictable—and she wouldn't have it any other way. Married to him, every day would be an adventure, one she would cherish.

THE EDITORS' CORNER

Along with May flowers come four fabulous LOVESWEPTs that will dazzle you with humor, excitement, and, above all, love. Touching, tender, packed with emotion and wonderfully happy endings, our four upcoming romances are real treasures.

Starting the lineup is the innovative Ruth Owen with **AND BABIES MAKE FOUR**, LOVESWEPT #786. Naked to the waist, his jeans molded to his thighs like a second skin, Sam Donovan looks like trouble—untamed and shameless! Dr. Noel Revere hadn't expected her guide to the island's sacred places to be so uncivilized, but this rebel sets her blood on fire and stirs her insides like a runaway hurricane. Can they survive a journey into the jungle shared by two matchmaking computers with mating on their minds? Once again,

Ruth Owen delivers an exotic adventure that is both wildly sexy and wickedly funny!

In her enchanting debut novel, **KISS AND TELL**, LOVESWEPT #787, Suzanne Brockmann adds a dash of mystery to a favorite romantic fantasy. When Dr. Marshall Devlin spots Leila Hunt alone on the dance floor, he yearns to charm the violet-eyed Cinderella into his arms, but how can he court the lady when they fight over everything, and always have? Then the clock strikes twelve and Leila is possessed by the passion of a familiar stranger. He captures her lips—and her soul—in a moment of magic, but can she learn to love the man behind the mask?

From award-winning author Terry Lawrence comes **FUGITIVE FATHER**, LOVESWEPT #788. A single light burned in the window of the isolated lakeside cottage, but Ben Renfield wondered which was the greater risk—hiding in the woods to evade his pursuers or seeking refuge with a beautiful stranger! Touched by his need, tempted by her own, Bridget Bernard trades precious solitude for perilous intimacy . . . and feels her own walls begin to crack. Can rescuing a lonely warrior transform her own destiny? Terry Lawrence blends simmering suspense and stunning sensuality in a tale that explores the tender mysteries of the human heart.

Finally, there's **STILL MR. & MRS.**, LOVESWEPT #789, by talented newcomer Patricia Olney. Two years before, they'd embraced in a heated moment, courted in one sultry afternoon, and wed in a reckless promise to cherish forever. Now Gabriel and Rebecca Stewart are days from the heart-breaking end of a dream! When a business crisis demands a last-minute lover's charade, Gabe offers Reb anything she wants—but will their seductive game of "let's pretend" ignite flames of dangerous desire? In this delicious story of second chances, Patricia Olney makes us believe in the enduring miracle of love.

Happy reading!

With warmest wishes,

Beth de Guzman
Shauna Summers

Beth de Guzman   Shauna Summers

Senior Editor   Editor

P.S. Watch for these Bantam women's fiction titles coming in April: From the *New York Times* bestselling author Betina Krahn comes another blockbuster romance filled with her patented brand of love and laughter in **THE UNLIKELY ANGEL.** Also welcome nationally bestselling author Iris Johansen in her hardcover debut of **THE UGLY DUCKLING,** a tale of contemporary romantic suspense! **DANGEROUS TO HOLD** by Elizabeth Thornton is filled with her trademark passion and suspense, and **THE REBEL AND THE REDCOAT** by Karyn

Monk promises a scorching tale of passion set against the dramatic backdrop of the American Revolution! Be sure to see next month's LOVESWEPTs for a preview of these exceptional novels. And immediately following this page, preview the Bantam women's fiction titles on sale now!

A tantalizing tale of a legendary knight and a headstrong lady whose daring quest for a mysterious crystal will draw them into a whirlwind of treachery—and desire.

From *New York Times* bestseller
Amanda Quick
comes

MYSTIQUE

When the fearsome knight called Hugh the Relentless swept into Lingwood Manor like a storm, everyone cowered—except Lady Alice. Sharp-tongued and unrepentant, the flame-haired beauty believed Sir Hugh was not someone to dread but the fulfillment of her dreams. She knew he had come for the dazzling green crystal, knew he would be displeased to find that it was no longer in her possession. Yet Alice had a proposition for the dark and forbidding knight: In return for a dowry that would free Alice and her brother from their uncle's grasp, she would lend her powers of detection to his warrior's skills and together they would recover his treasured stone. But even as Hugh accepted her terms, he added a condition of his own: Lady Alice must agree to a temporary betrothal—one that would soon draw her deep into Hugh's great stone fortress, and into a battle that could threaten their lives . . . and their only chance at love.

From the winner of the Romantic Times *Storyteller of the Year Award comes*

DIABLO

by **Patricia Potter**

Raised in a notorious outlaw hideout, Nicky Thompson learned to shoot fast, ride hard, and hold her own against killers and thieves. Yet nothing in her experience prepared her for the new brand of danger that just rode in. Ruggedly handsome, with an easy strength and a hint of deviltry in his smile, Diablo made Nicky's heart race not with fright but with a sizzling arousal. When she challenged him to taste her womanly charms, she didn't know he was a condemned convict who'd come to Sanctuary with one secret purpose—to destroy it in exchange for pardons for himself and a friend. Would a renegade hungry for freedom jeopardize his dangerous mission for a last chance at love?

With a sigh of pure contentment, Kane relaxed in the big tin bathtub in an alcove off the barber's shop. One hand rubbed his newly shaved cheek. The barber had been good, the water hot. The shave had been sheer luxury, costing five times what it would have in any other town, but that didn't bother him. In truth, it amused him. He was spending Marshal Ben Masters's money.

He lit a long, thin cigar that he'd purchased, also at a rather high price. He supposed he was as close to heaven as he was apt to get. Sinking deeper into the water, he tried not to think beyond this immediate pleasure. But he couldn't forget his friend Davy. The leash, as Masters so coldly called it, pulled tight around his neck.

Reluctantly, he rose from the tub and pulled on the new clothes he'd purchased at the general store. Blue denim trousers, a dark blue shirt. A clean bandanna around his neck. The old one had been beyond redemption. He ran a comb through his freshly washed hair, trying to tame it, and regarded himself briefly in the mirror. The scar stood out. It was one of the few he'd earned honorably, but it was like a brand, forever identifying him as Diablo.

Hell, what difference did it make? He wasn't here to court. He was here to betray. He couldn't forget that. Not for a single moment.

With a snort of self-disgust, he left the room for the stable. He would explore the boundaries of Sanctuary, do a reconnaissance. He had experience at that. Lots of experience.

Nicky rode for an hour before she heard gunshots.

She headed toward the sound, knowing full well that a stray bullet could do as much damage as a directed one. Her brother Robin was crouching, a gunbelt wrapped around his lean waist, his hand on the grip of a six-shooter. In a quick movement, he pulled it from the holster and aimed at a target affixed to a tree. Then he saw Nicky.

The pride on his face faltered, and then he set his jaw rebelliously and fired. He missed.

Nicky turned her attention to the man next to him. Arrogance radiated from him as he leered at her. Her skin crawling, she rode over to them and addressed Cobb Yancy. "If my uncle knew about this, you would be out of Sanctuary faster than a bullet from that gun."

"That so, honey?" Yancy drawled. "Then he'd have to do something about your baby brother, wouldn't he?" He took the gun from Robin and stood there, letting it dangle from his fingers.

Nicky held out her hand. "Give me the gun."

"Why don't you take it from me?" Yancy's voice was low, inviting.

"You leave now, and I'll forget about this," she said.

"What if I don't want you to forget about it?" he asked, moving toward her horse. "The boy can take your horse back. You can ride with me." His hand was suddenly on the horse's halter.

"Robin can walk back," she said, trying to back Molly. Yancy's grasp, though, was too strong.

Yancy turned to Robin. "You do that, boy. Start walking."

Robin looked from Yancy to Nicky and back again, apprehension beginning to show in his face. "I'd rather ride back with you, Mr. Yancy."

The gun was suddenly pointed at Robin. "Do as I say. Your sister and I will be along later."

Nicky was stiff with anger and not a little fear. "My uncle will kill you," Nicky pointed out.

"He may try," Yancy said. "I've been wondering if he's as fast as everyone says."

Nicky knew then that Cobb Yancy had just been looking for an excuse to try her uncle. Had he scented weakness? Was he after Sanctuary?

She felt for the small derringer she'd tucked inside a pocket in her trousers. "Go on, Robin," she said. "I'll catch up to you."

Robin didn't move.

"Go," she ordered in a voice that had gone hard.

Softness didn't survive here, not in these mountains, not among these men.

Instead of obeying her, Robin lunged for the gun in Yancy's hand. It went off, and Robin went down. Nicky aimed her derringer directly at Yancy's heart and fired.

He looked stunned as the gun slipped from his fingers and he went down on his knees, then toppled over. Nicky dismounted and ran over to Robin. Blood was seeping from a wound in his shoulder.

She heard hoofbeats and grabbed the gun Yancy had been holding. It could be his brother coming.

But it wasn't. It was Diablo, looking very different than he had earlier. He reined in his horse at the sight of the gun aimed in his direction. His gaze moved from her to Robin to the body on the ground.

"Trouble?"

"Nothing I can't handle," Nicky said, keeping the gun pointed at him.

The side of his mouth turned up by the scar inched higher. "I see you can," he said, then studied Robin. "What about him?"

"My brother," she explained stiffly. "That polecat shot him."

"I think he needs some help."

"Not from you, mister," she said.

His brows knitted together, and he shifted in the saddle. Then ignoring the threat in her hand, he slid down from his horse and walked over to Robin, pulling the boy's shirt back to look at the wound.

Robin grimaced, then fixed his concentration on Diablo's scar. "You're that new one," he said. "Diablo."

Diablo nodded. "Some call me that. How in the hell did everyone around know I was coming?"

"There's not many secrets here," Robin said, but his voice was strained. He was obviously trying to be brave for the gunslinger. Nicky sighed. Hadn't he learned anything today?

Diablo studied the wound a moment, then took off his bandanna and gave it to Robin. "It's clean. Hold it to the wound to stop the bleeding."

He then went over to Cobb Yancy, checked for signs of life and found none. He treated death very casually, Nicky noticed. "He's dead, all right," Diablo said.

Before she could protest, he returned to Robin. He helped Robin shed his shirt, which he tore in two and made into a sling. When he was through, he offered a steadying arm to Robin.

"Don't," Nicky said sharply. "I'll help him."

"He's losing blood," Diablo said. "He could lose consciousness. You prepared to take his whole weight?"

Nicky studied her brother's face. It was pale, growing paler by the moment. "We'll send someone back for Yancy. He has a brother. It would be best not to meet him."

Diablo didn't ask any questions, she'd give him that. She looked down at her hands and noticed they were shaking. She'd never killed a man before.

Diablo's eyes seemed to stab through her, reading her thoughts. Then he was guiding Robin to Yancy's horse, practically lifting her brother onto the gelding. There was an easy strength about him, a confidence, that surprised Nicky. He'd looked so much the renegade loner that morning, yet here he'd taken charge automatically, as if he were used to leadership. Resentment mixed with gratitude.

She tucked the gun into the waist of her trousers

and mounted her mare. She kept seeing Yancy's surprised face as he went down. Her hands were shaking even more now. She'd killed a man. A man who had a very dangerous brother.

She had known this would happen one day. But nothing could have prepared her for the despair she felt at taking someone's life. She felt sick inside.

Diablo, who was riding ahead with Robin, looked back. He reined in his own horse until she was abreast of him, and she felt his watchful gaze settle on her. "Tell Yancy's brother I did it."

Nothing he could have said would have surprised her more.

"Why?"

"I can take care of myself."

He couldn't have insulted her more. "And what do you think *I* just did?"

"I think you just killed your first man, and you don't need another on your conscience. You certainly don't need it on your stomach. You look like you're going to upchuck."

She glared at him. "I'm fine."

"Good. Your brother isn't."

All of Nicky's attention went to Robin. He was swaying in his saddle. She moved her horse around to his side. "Just a few more minutes, Robin. Hold on."

"I'm sorry, Sis. I shouldn't have gone with . . . Cobb Yancy, but—"

"Hush," she said. "If you hadn't, Yancy would have found something else. He was after more than me."

But Robin wasn't listening. He was holding on to the saddle horn for dear life, and his face was a white mask now.

"Maybe I should ride ahead," she said. "Get some help."

"You got a doctor in this place?" Diablo asked.

"Not right now. But Andy—"

"Andy?"

"The blacksmith. He knows some medicine, and I can sew up a wound."

"Go on ahead and get him ready," Diablo ordered. "I'll get your brother there." He stopped his horse, slipped off, and then mounted behind Robin, holding him upright in the saddle.

Could she really trust Diablo that much? Dare she leave him alone with Robin?

"I'll take care of him," Diablo said, more gently this time.

Nicky finally nodded and spurred her mare into a gallop.

Wearing it was just asking for trouble

THE BAD LUCK WEDDING DRESS

The most memorable Texas romance yet
from the uniquely talented

Geralyn Dawson

"One of the best new authors to come along in years—fresh, charming, and romantic!"
—*New York Times* bestselling author Jill Barnett

They were calling it the Bad Luck Wedding Dress, and Jenny Fortune knew that spelled trouble for her Fort Worth dressmaking shop. Just because the Bailey girls had met with one mishap or another after wearing Jenny's loveliest creation, her clientele had begun to stay away in droves. Yet Jenny was still betting she could turn her luck around—by wearing the gown herself at her very own wedding. There's just one hitch: first she has to find a groom. . . .

While people all over the world have strange ideas about luck, Fort Worth, being a gambling town, seemed to have stranger ideas than most. Folks here made bets on everything, from the weather to the length of the sermon at the Baptist church on Sunday. Jenny theorized that this practice contributed to a dedicated belief in the vagaries of luck, making it easy for many to lay the blame for the Baileys' difficulties on the dress.

Monique shrugged. "Well, I think you're wrong. Give it a try, dear. It's a perfect solution. And you needn't be overly concerned with your lack of a beau. Despite your father's influence, you are still my daughter. The slightest of efforts will offer you plenty of men from whom to choose. Now, I think you should start with this."

She pulled the pins from Jenny's chignon, fluffed out her wavy blond tresses, then pressed a kiss to her cheek. "I'm so glad I was able to help, dear. Now I'd best get back to the station. Keep me informed about the developments, and if you choose to follow my advice, be sure to telegraph me with the date of the wedding. I'll do my best to see that your father drags his nose from his studies long enough to attend."

"Wait, Monique," Jenny began. But the dressing-room curtains flapped in her mother's wake, and the front door's welcome bell tinkled before she could get out the words "I can't do these back buttons myself."

Wonderful. Simply wonderful. She closed her eyes and sighed. It'd be just her luck if not a single woman entered the shop this afternoon. "The Bad Luck Wedding Dress strikes again," she grumbled.

Of course she didn't believe it. Jenny didn't believe in luck, not to the extent many others did, anyway. People could be lucky, but not things. A dress could not be unlucky any more than a rabbit's foot could be lucky. "What's the saying?" she murmured aloud, eyeing her reflection in the mirror. "The rabbit's foot wasn't too lucky for the rabbit?"

Jenny set to work twisting and contorting her body, and eventually she managed all but two of the buttons. Grimacing, she gave the taffeta a jerk and felt the dress fall free even as she heard the buttons plunk against the floor.

While she gave little credit to luck, she did believe rather strongly in fate. As she stepped out of the wedding gown and donned her own dress, she considered the role fate had played in leading her to this moment. It was fate that she'd chosen to make Fort Worth her home. Fate that the Baileys had chosen her to make the dress. Fate that the brides had suffered accidents.

The shop's bell sounded. "*Now* someone comes," she whispered grumpily. "Not while I'm stuck in a five-hundred-dollar dress and needing assistance." She stooped to pick the buttons up off the floor and immediately felt contrite. She'd best be grateful for any customer, and besides, she welcomed the distraction from her troublesome thoughts.

Pasting a smile on her face, Jenny exited the dressing room and spied Mr. Trace McBride entering her shop.

He was dressed in work clothes—black frock jacket and black trousers, white shirt beneath a gold satin vest. He carried a black felt hat casually in his hand and raked a hand nervously through thick, dark hair.

Immediately, she ducked back behind the curtain.

Oh, my. Her heart began to pound. Why would the one man in Fort Worth, Texas, who stirred her imagination walk into her world at this particular moment?

She swallowed hard as she thought of her mother's advice. It was a crazy thought. Ridiculous.

But maybe, considering the stakes, it wouldn't hurt to explore the idea. Jenny had the sudden image of herself clothed in the Bad Luck Wedding Dress, standing beside Trace McBride, his three darling daughters looking on as she repeated vows to a preacher.

Her mouth went dry. Hadn't she sworn to fight for Fortune's Design? Wasn't she willing to do whatever it took to save her shop? If that meant marriage, well . . .

Wasn't it better to give up the dream of true love than the security of her independence?

Jenny stared at her reflection in the mirror. What would it hurt to explore her mother's idea? She wouldn't be committing to anything.

Jenny recalled the lessons she'd learned at Monique's knees. Flirtation. Seduction. That's how it was done. She took a deep breath. Was she sure about this? Could she go through with it? She *was* Monique Day's daughter. Surely that should count for something. She could do this.

Maybe.

Trace McBride. What did she really know about him? He was a businessman, saloon keeper, landlord, father. His smile made her warm inside and the musky, masculine scent of him haunted her mind. Once when he'd taken her arm in escort, she couldn't help but notice the steel of his muscles beneath the cover of his coat. His fingers would be rough against the softness of her skin. His kiss would be—

Jenny startled. Oh, bother. Had she lost her sense entirely?

Perhaps she had. She was seriously considering her mother's idea.

What was she thinking? He'd never noticed her before; what made her think he'd notice her now? What made her think he'd even consider such a fate as marriage?

Fate. There was that word again.

Was Trace McBride her fate? Could he save her from the rumor of the Bad Luck Wedding Dress? Could he help her save Fortune's Design?

She wouldn't know unless she did a little exploring. Was she brave enough, woman enough, to try?

She was Jenny Fortune. What more was there to say?

Taking a deep breath, Jenny pinched her cheeks, fluffed her honey-colored hair, and walked out into the shop.

OFFICIAL RULES  **NO PURCHASE NECESSARY**

To enter the sweepstakes outlined below, you must respond by the date specified and follow all entry instructions published elsewhere in this offer.

DREAM COME TRUE SWEEPSTAKES

Sweepstakes begins 9/1/94, ends 1/15/96. To qualify for the Early Bird Prize, entry must be received by the date specified elsewhere in this offer. Winners will be selected in random drawings on 2/29/96 by an independent judging organization whose decisions are final. Early Bird winner will be selected in a separate drawing from among all qualifying entries.

Odds of winning determined by total number of entries received. Distribution not to exceed 300 million.

Estimated maximum retail value of prizes: Grand (1) $25,000 (cash alternative $20,000); First (1) $2,000; Second (1) $750; Third (50) $75; Fourth (1,000) $50; Early Bird (1) $5,000. Total prize value: $86,500.

Automobile and travel trailer must be picked up at a local dealer; all other merchandise prizes will be shipped to winners. Awarding of any prize to a minor will require written permission of parent/guardian. If a trip prize is won by a minor, s/he must be accompanied by parent/legal guardian. Trip prizes subject to availability and must be completed within 12 months of date awarded. Blackout dates may apply. Early Bird trip is on a space available basis and does not include port charges, gratuities, optional shore excursions and onboard personal purchases. Prizes are not transferable or redeemable for cash except as specified. No substitution for prizes except as necessary due to unavailability. Travel trailer and/or automobile license and registration fees are winners' responsibility as are any other incidental expenses not specified herein.

Early Bird Prize may not be offered in some presentations of this sweepstakes. Grand through third prize winners will have the option of selecting any prize offered at level won. All prizes will be awarded. Drawing will be held at 204 Center Square Road, Bridgeport, NJ 08014. Winners need not be present. For winners list (available in June, 1996), send a self-addressed, stamped envelope by 1/15/96 to: Dream Come True Winners, P.O. Box 572, Gibbstown, NJ 08027.

THE FOLLOWING APPLIES TO THE SWEEPSTAKES ABOVE:

No purchase necessary. No photocopied or mechanically reproduced entries will be accepted. Not responsible for lost, late, misdirected, damaged, incomplete, illegible, or postage-die mail. Entries become the property of sponsors and will not be returned.

Winner(s) will be notified by mail. Winner(s) may be required to sign and return an affidavit of eligibility/release within 14 days of date on notification or an alternate may be selected. Except where prohibited by law, entry constitutes permission to use of winners' names, hometowns, and likenesses for publicity without additional compensation. Void where prohibited or restricted. All federal, state, provincial, and local laws and regulations apply.

All prize values are in U.S. currency. Presentation of prizes may vary; values at a given prize level will be approximately the same. All taxes are winners' responsibility.

Canadian residents, in order to win, must first correctly answer a time-limited skill testing question administered by mail. Any litigation regarding the conduct and awarding of a prize in this publicity contest by a resident of the province of Quebec may be submitted to the Regie des loteries et courses du Quebec.

Sweepstakes is open to legal residents of the U.S., Canada, and Europe (in those areas where made available) who have received this offer.

Sweepstakes in sponsored by Ventura Associates, 1211 Avenue of the Americas, New York, NY 10036 and presented by independent businesses. Employees of these, their advertising agencies and promotional companies involved in this promotion, and their immediate families, agents, successors, and assignees shall be ineligible to participate in the promotion and shall not be eligible for any prizes covered herein. SWP 3/95